THE LAST PRINCESS

A NOVEL BY

GALAXY CRAZE

poppy

LITTLE, BROWN AND COMPANY

New York   Boston

Poppy

Hachette Book Group
237 Park Avenue, New York, NY 10017
For more of your favorite series and novels, visit our website at www.pickapoppy.com

Poppy is an imprint of Little, Brown and Company.
The Poppy name and logo are trademarks of Hachette Book Group, Inc.

The publisher is not responsible for websites (or their contents) that are not owned by the publisher.

First Paperback Edition: April 2013
First published in hardcover in May 2012 by Little, Brown and Company

Library of Congress Cataloging-in-Publication Data

Craze, Galaxy.
The last princess / Galaxy Craze.
  p. cm.
  Summary: Tired of the royal family's relative comfort while they suffer in the wake of worldwide catastrophes in 2090, rebels kill the British king and abduct two of his children, but Princess Eliza escapes, disguises herself, and joins the rebels to seek revenge and the safe return of her siblings.
  ISBN 978-0-316-18548-6 (hc) / ISBN 978-0-316-18547-9 (pb)
  [1. Princesses—Fiction. 2. Revolutionaries—Fiction. 3. Kidnapping—Fiction. 4. Environmental degradation—Fiction. 5. England—Fiction.] I. Title.
  PZ7.C85982Las 2012
  [Fic]—dc23
                        2011042735

alloyentertainment
Produced by Alloy Entertainment
151 West 26th Street, New York, NY 10001

10 9 8 7 6 5 4 3 2

RRD-C

Printed in the United States of America

To Rowan

And to my editors, Joelle Hobeika and Cindy Eagan

Prologue

THE DAY BEGAN AS A BEAUTIFUL AND VIVID DREAM. IT WAS ONE of those rare days when the sun was out, and the light was soft and warm, Easter yellow. We were in the garden, just my mother and me; Mary had gone out with our father, but my mother was eight months pregnant and tired, so I had stayed to keep her company.

"*Oh.*" Mother rested her hands on her pregnant belly. We had packed a picnic, with bamboo mats and a lime-green gingham tablecloth and a few pillows to lie on. "I think your brother wants to join us."

I was reaching for her belly to feel my brother moving when we heard our butler, Rupert, calling to us. There was a delivery.

Standing at the doorway was a handsome man with

golden-blond curls. In his arms he held a basket of fresh, perfectly ripe fruit: peaches and plums, apricots and apples, deep red strawberries. I hadn't tasted fruit since the Seventeen Days.

"Who is it from?" my mother asked, unable to take her eyes from the gift.

The man smiled as he handed over the basket, revealing a row of perfectly white teeth. I remember staring at his teeth, thinking they looked plastic.

"Long live the queen," he said, and she smiled as he backed out the door. My mother had always been embarrassed by the expression.

We carried the basket outside to the blanket and sat down in the emerald grass.

Mother reached into the basket and plucked out a perfect-looking peach. She brought it to her nose, closing her eyes as she breathed in its scent.

"Look, there's a card inside." I plucked a small white note from the pile of strawberries, and read it aloud.

To the royal family and the new baby. Enjoy.
—C.H.

"Who is C.H.?" Mother asked.

I ignored her, distracted by the fruit, wondering what to try first: a plum? A strawberry?

My mother opened her mouth, biting into the peach. A drop of juice rolled down her chin.

"Oh, it's delicious. It's the most delicious thing I've ever tasted." As she took another bite, her serene smile turned to a look of concern. She plucked something off her tongue and placed it on her palm. "But peaches don't have seeds," she said.

I leaned forward, looking at her hand; in it lay a tiny metal star.

My mother's face drained of color as she fell back onto the blanket, her hands clawing at the grass, her fingernails digging into the earth. In the breeze, I heard a rasping sound.

It was my mother's last breath.

1

CAREFULLY, I UNCLASPED THE LOCKET FROM MY NECK, LETTING the weight of the Welsh gold fall into the palm of my hand. It was the end of August, but it was cool inside the castle's thick stone walls. Even in summer, a draft wafted through its rooms like a lonely ghost.

I opened the locket and stared at the miniature portrait of my mother, then at my reflection in the window's leaded glass, then back again, until my eyes blurred. We had the same dark hair and light blue eyes. Would I grow up to look like her? I closed my eyes, trying to feel her arms around me, hear the low murmur of her voice, smell the rose oil she dabbed on the inside of her wrists every morning. But the memories weren't coming back as clearly today. I snapped the locket shut and wiped away my tears.

I could stare at my reflection all day, but I would never recognize myself. I would never be the girl I was before the Seventeen Days, before my mother was killed. My family had grown hollow inside, like an old tree dead at the roots but still standing. Our hearts were broken.

They never caught Cornelius Hollister, the man who had killed my mother. He haunted my dreams. His blond hair, his intense blue eyes, his gleaming white teeth followed me down darkened streets while I slept. Sometimes I dreamed I was killing him, stabbing him in the heart over and over again, until I woke up drenched in sweat, my hands clenched in fists. Then I would curl up and weep for what I had lost, and what I had found in myself during those dreams.

Outside Balmoral Castle, a gray veil of rain fell over the barren landscape. The color of the rain had changed since the Seventeen Days. It was no longer clear and soft like teardrops. This rain was gray, sometimes dark as soot. And it was bitter cold.

I watched the soldiers circling the courtyard, rain beading off their heavy black rain gear. Round, half-empty ammunition belts hung around their necks, carefully protected from the weather. No cartridge could be wasted with ammunition so low. Like the bags of flour in the pantry, the jars of oats, the salted snakes and pigeons hanging in the larder—nothing could be wasted. Everything, scarce.

A thick dust swirled through the air, marking the sky like a bruise. Six years ago, everything had changed. For seventeen straight days, the world was battered by earth-splitting quakes, torrential hurricanes, tornadoes, and tsunamis. Volcanoes erupted, filling the sky with fiery smoke that blocked out the sun and covered the fields with strange purple ash that suffocated crops.

Scientists called it a catastrophic coincidence. Zealots said it was the act of a vengeful God, punishing us for polluting His universe. But I just remembered it as one of the last times I had my mother with me. We spent those seventeen days in the bomb shelter below Buckingham Palace, along with government aides and palace staff, holding each other tight as the world shattered around us. Only my mother kept calm. She was in constant motion, passing out blankets and canned soup, her soft voice reassuring everyone that it would be okay.

When we finally came to the surface, everything had changed.

I missed the light the most. The watery early-morning

sunshine, the hot blaze of a summer afternoon, the sparkle of Christmas tree lights, even the soft glow of a naked light-bulb. We emerged from the dark into smoke and ashes, into a world lit by fire.

I felt something cold on my hand and looked down to see my dog, Bella, staring up at me with her large, dark eyes. I had found her with Polly, the groundskeeper's daughter and my best friend, shivering under the garden shed when she was just a tiny puppy. We had fed her milk from a doll's bottle and nursed her back to health.

"Let me guess—you want to go for a walk. Even in this soaking rain?" My voice sounded quiet in the high-ceilinged bedroom.

Bella wagged her tail in excitement, looking up hopefully.

"Okay, in a minute. But I have to finish packing first, or Mary will nag me to death."

Bella barked again, as though she understood. My suit-case lay open on the four-poster bed, under the shade of a white eyelet canopy. This was our last day in Scotland. We were taking the train to London this afternoon to make it home in time for the Roses Ball tomorrow. The annual Roses Ball marked the traditional opening of Government Offices and Parliament after the summer recess, and my father always made a speech. Even though I hated leaving Scotland, I was ready to see him again. This was the first summer he hadn't spent at least part of the holiday with us. He kept sending notes with the Carriers, saying that he was busy with the rebuilding projects and would visit as soon as he could, but he never did.

After our mother was killed, my father had retreated from the world. Once, right after it happened, I found him alone in his office in the middle of the night. Without turning to look at me, he said, "I wish I had eaten the peach. It should have been me. That poison was meant for me."

I grabbed my hairbrush, my toothbrush, my pajamas, and my book, quickly throwing them into the suitcase. It wasn't exactly neat, but it would do.

Bella barked impatiently by the door. "I'm hurrying." I grabbed my raincoat from the hook on the wall, slipped my feet into a pair of bright yellow Wellingtons, and ran into the hallway.

I knocked softly on Jamie's door but didn't wait for a response before opening it. Inside, the curtains were drawn; only a hazy line of light crept in to illuminate the dark room. The astringent smell of Jamie's medicine hung in the stifling air. A small cup of the deceivingly cheerful cherry-red syrup sat untouched on his bedside table, next to a bowl of oatmeal and a cold chamomile tea. It was already midday and he hadn't taken his medicine yet?

My younger brother had barely made it into the world. After our mother was poisoned, the doctors had to force his birth surgically. He survived, but his blood had been tainted by the mysterious poison. It would be with him, slowly killing him from the inside, for the rest of his life.

Our sister, Mary, had made Jamie stay in his room most of the summer, bundled up against the constant drafty dampness so he wouldn't risk catching a cold. She had the best intentions, but I knew how depressed he felt, trapped inside. Today was his last chance to be outside in the fresh air before returning to the smog-filled London streets.

I walked over to where Jamie lay sleeping under the covers. I hated to wake him, especially from what seemed to be a peaceful sleep. The medicine kept him alive but also stole his energy and fogged his thoughts. Worst of all, it gave him terrible nightmares.

I gently turned back the pale blue comforter with pictures of the planets on it. "Jamie?" I whispered. But the bed was empty.

I was about to turn away when I spotted the corner of his writing pad hidden beneath the pillow. The book where he drew intricate drawings of what he imagined the world looked like before the Seventeen Days. The animals were far too big, the cars looked like spaceships, and the colors were all off, but Mary and I never had the heart to tell him. So what if he imagined the world from before as a wonderful, impossible place? It wasn't as though he would ever get to see it.

I turned the page of the notebook to his most recent entry, and my heart started to beat faster.

31 August

Last night I heard two of the housekeepers talking in the kitchen. They said my name and I stopped to listen. I know I shouldn't eavesdrop. They said how worried my father and sister are about me. How difficult it is to get my medicine now and how expensive and hard to find it is. They could do so much good for the people with the petrol and ammunition they have to trade for it. They said I'm a burden to my family.

I'm sick and useless. The doctors say I won't live much longer anyway. I can't stay here. I don't want to be a burden anymore.

2

I RACED DOWN THE LONG HALLWAY TO THE BACK STAIRCASE, Bella following close at my heels. I jumped down the stone steps three, four at a time, keeping one hand on the banister for balance.

My Wellingtons squelched in the mud as I ran down the winding trail to the stables. Only three horses were out to pasture, and Jamie's mare, Luna, was missing. Hurrying, I unlatched the wooden gate to the field.

"Jasper! Quick, quick!" I called to my horse. There was no time to bother with a saddle or reins, but I'd been riding bareback on Jasper since I could walk. I clambered up onto his back and turned toward the woods. We were almost out the gate when I saw a pale green cardigan looped over the post. It was Jamie's. He must have left it when the rain stopped. I felt an immediate pang of relief. He hadn't been gone long, and on gentle old Luna, he couldn't have gotten far.

If he was in the woods, I'd need a weapon. The Roamers could be out there. I grabbed the only thing I could find, an old knife with a broken leather-bound handle. I could throw it or, if I had to, fight with it. After the Seventeen Days, without phones or computers or television, Mary and I amused ourselves play-fighting with the Royal Swords. The Master of Arms gave us lessons, teaching us to slash, stab, and parry. Mary and I would fence against each other, betting on the little luxuries that were still left over from before: a square of Cadbury chocolate, a piece of spearmint gum. Later, when the government food rations were gone, we would take spears and throwing knives to the woods around Balmoral, hunting the snakes and pigeons and few other creatures that remained. I was surprised to find that I had quite good aim, unlike Mary, who never could get the hang of throwing a knife.

"Bella, come!" I held out the sweater for her to sniff. Bella could catch almost any scent you gave her. Polly and I had trained her one summer, hiding things in the woods—a toy, a shirt, an old shoe—rewarding her with a treat when she found them. Bella sniffed the sweater up and down. "Track," I said firmly.

She placed her nose to the ground. After a few seconds, she took off running toward the fields.

The brown earth blurred beneath me as Jasper galloped behind Bella. I leaned forward and wrapped my arms around his neck, closing my eyes. I hated seeing my woods like this. The Seventeen Days had transformed the sun-drenched forest of my childhood into a dark, tangled place. Most woodland animals had died in the destruction, or were later hunted to extinction by the Roamers. Only the worms, leeches, and snakes were left. The ground was covered with gnarled, rotting tree roots, spreading out in every direction like giant hands.

I pulled Jasper to a stop at the top of the hill, scanning the woods for signs of the Roamers—smoke, fire pits, grave markers. Or worse, the hearts of their prey, human and animal, mounted on sticks. The Roamers had banded together after the Seventeen Days, when electric security in the prisons failed and the inmates were able to escape. They gathered in the woods, eating anything they could kill. Since most wild animals were dead, they hunted humans. You could tell a Roamer camp by the sickly sweet smell of roasting human flesh.

I felt something brush against my forehead and looked up. It was a frayed rope, hung from a high branch. The base was knotted to the tree, a piece of webbing left hooked on a branch. A trap. I fingered the edge of the rope, looking for footprints. They were there, clear outlines in the mud.

"Go!" I shouted to Jasper, trying not to think of Jamie caught in a web of rope. Bella raced up the logging trail along the side of the hill. Finally, I spotted Jamie's small figure in the distance, hunched over on Luna, riding deeper into the woods.

"Jamie!" I yelled, even though I knew the Roamers might hear us. "Jamie, stop!" He paused but didn't turn around. The small backpack on his shoulders was filled to bursting, and I wondered what he had packed for the outside world. A pillow? A flashlight? I spurred Jasper on, and quickly reached Jamie and Luna.

I slid off Jasper and ventured closer. "Jamie," I said softly. "Please come home."

He turned to look at me. Dark circles like bruises spread below his blue eyes, which were sunk into the hollows of his face. His skin was white as rice paper, and in the dim light of the forest, he seemed almost translucent.

"I don't want to be a burden anymore," he said simply, his voice so weak it was nearly lost.

I took a step closer. "You can't just leave us." My words sounded awkward and slight, even to me. "You can't just give up."

"You don't know what it's like," he said. "You'll never understand."

"You're right, I can't possibly understand." I choked back a sob. I had no idea what he suffered every day. "But think of all the pain you'll cause everyone by leaving us. Think of Father, think of Mary. Please stay . . . for me?" I held out my hand.

Jamie slid down from his horse and took a step toward me. Out of the corner of my eye, I saw a wisp of smoke rising above the trees in the distance. I stiffened, pressing my fingers to my lips so that he would know to be quiet.

I heard the deep rumbling of men's voices. A strange whirring. The sound of a motor starting. Jamie stared up at me, his eyes wide. "What is it?" he whispered.

I shook my head and took his hand. He didn't know about the Roamers; Mary and I had tried to protect him from the world's worst horrors. We ran for the granite rock at the edge of the clearing and crawled underneath. I held Bella in my lap, grabbing her snout with both hands so she wouldn't bark. One sound and we would be caught. Jasper's ears pricked up as if he sensed the danger. He and Luna trotted into the woods and vanished from sight just in time.

A band of men entered the clearing just a few yards away. They were dressed in tattered gray prison uniforms, the words "MaxSec" tattooed in coarse black letters on their foreheads. A few had guns. Most carried makeshift weapons: hooks, chains, gardening shears, bludgeons, old pipes filed down and sharpened to points, and what appeared to be a hedge trimmer that had been stripped of its casing so that the blade rotated menacingly. Two of the men carried a thick branch between them. A sack, soaked red with blood, hung from it heavily.

I tried to cover Jamie's eyes with my hands, but I knew he had seen. He had seen the worst of humanity. *Don't look over here, don't look over here*, I thought desperately. If the Roamers gave the rock a second glance, they would notice the shadowy area underneath and come looking for us. We would be as good as dead.

I tried to hold Bella close, but in a burst of strength she wriggled away from me and sprinted toward the men, barking aggressively. I wanted to call her back, but I bit my lips until I tasted blood.

The two men carrying the bloodied bundle stopped and laid the branch down on the ground. One of them stepped forward, aiming his pistol into the darkness of the surrounding forest.

"Who's there?" he called.

I pressed closer to the rock, holding my breath.

"Stop jumping at nothing," the second man told him. "It's just a wild dog. A dirty old mutt."

The man with the gun turned toward Bella. He was missing one eye, a metal plate covering the empty socket.

"Come on, the others are ahead of us," the second man complained. "Can't waste the bullet on a stringy, skinny dog. We've got other food needs eating." The first man lowered his gun with a sigh. They lifted the branch and its bloodied cargo onto their shoulders and started walking into the distance.

Jamie and I waited under the rock, holding each other and shaking. When I finally smelled the sickly sweet burning smell, I knew we could make our escape.

3

THE SUN WAS FINALLY STARTING TO EMERGE FROM BEHIND THE heavy blanket of clouds when we returned to Balmoral Castle.

"Eliza! Jamie!" Mary's voice rang out in the still air.

"You can't tell her," I reminded my younger brother. "You promised."

"I know," he said, his voice shaking.

"Jamie, I need you to know something." I pulled Luna's reins toward me so our horses were side by side. "You have to understand that people didn't used to eat other people. Before the Seventeen Days, there was no such thing as the Roamers. You have to believe things will get better." I thought of him alone in those woods. "You know there are good people in the world. That's *our* side. If we give up, if we run away, then the bad people win."

Jamie nodded, his eyes wide. Mary galloped toward us, pulling the reins fiercely to reach a sudden stop. Her long blonde hair fell around her face, and her ivory complexion was flushed from the wind and exercise.

"Where have you been?" she yelled, looking from me to Jamie. "I've been looking everywhere. The train is leaving in an hour. Did you forget we were going back today?"

"Mary, I—"

"Jamie! You know better than to leave your room," she said, ignoring my protests. "You have to take care of yourself!"

She swung back to me, her eyes narrowing. "How could you let this happen?"

"I know, it's my fault," I said, fighting the urge to break down and tell her everything that had happened. "We wanted to have a nice last day . . ."

"No, it's my fault," Jamie interrupted. "I begged Eliza to let me go riding."

"While I did all the cleaning and packing as usual." She sighed. "I hope you didn't go near the woods."

"Of course not! Just the fields." I hated lying to Mary, but sometimes I had no choice.

Mary looked at me, the frown between her eyes softening. "Do you know what it's like for me, always having to take care of you?"

"You're not our mother!" I said angrily, immediately regretting it.

"Someone has to be the mother here," Mary replied quietly. I wanted to apologize, but she was already riding away.

On my way back to the castle, I saw George, our grounds-keeper. He had unlocked the steel doors of the gardening shed and unwound the thick metal chain holding them shut. The petrol tanks were in there, guarded by shepherd dogs, as protected as we could keep them without electricity.

The black Jeep we always drove to the train station stood next to the shed. I watched as George tipped the end of the gasoline spout into its tank, a grim look on his face. Even from where I stood, I could hear the slow *drip-drip-drip* of the gasoline.

"It's almost gone?"

George turned toward me, and I noticed for the first time how he had aged this summer. There was a hollowness in his cheeks, a troubled look in his eyes that hadn't used to be there.

"They should get the rigs mended soon enough," George said, which we both knew was a lie.

"We can take the horses. They don't need oil."

I was trying to make a joke, but George didn't laugh. "We have enough for this trip. The roads are too dangerous to go in an open carriage and risk the horses getting stolen."

I looked over at the Jeep. It was made of bulletproof steel and glass, but George had added an extra layer of steel over the windows. Shields of metal now protected the tires, and sharp spikes had been welded to the roof and sides. He had also sanded away the W that stood for Windsor. Without it, I realized, no one would know us. Ever since my mother's death, my father had refused to let us appear in public or even to circulate royal portraits. Only our name was recognizable.

"Is it the Roamers?" I asked.

"The Roamers don't go on the roads."

"Then what's all this for?"

"Just extra protection. Don't worry your pretty head about it," he said, turning away from me to pour the last of the petrol in the Jeep.

I shook off the comment, knowing George didn't mean to offend me, and continued on. "Who was in the kitchen last night? Late?"

George looked at me curiously. "Why?"

"One of the staff called Jamie a burden. He heard her say it. Find out who it was. Please," I added, in as polite and princesslike a voice as I could muster. "It nearly killed him hearing her say that."

The door of my room creaked as I pushed it open. The girl at my writing desk turned around, her blue eyes wide with surprise.

"Eliza!" Polly jumped up out of the chair, holding a piece of paper behind her back. "I thought you were out riding." Her voice wavered with unshed tears.

"What's the matter?" I said, walking toward her. Her hand shook as she kept the paper hidden from my sight.

"Nothing." She forced a smile. "I was just writing you a good-bye note. Not finished yet."

"I'll miss you so much, Polly." I drew my best friend in for a close hug, blinking back tears of my own.

We heard footsteps approaching the door, and Clara walked in. "Eliza, honey, it's time to go." She was carrying a basket of food and a blanket. "I've packed you some sandwiches for the train."

I leaned in to give Polly's mother a big hug. She'd been like a second mother to me ever since my own died. Wrapped in her arms, her rough wool sweater scratching my cheek, I felt safe.

"Eliza! Hurry!" I heard Mary's voice from the courtyard. Polly and I rolled our eyes at each other as we grabbed my luggage and raced down the stairs, starting to laugh.

In the courtyard, Mary was standing at the door to the Jeep, tapping her foot in impatience. I was surprised to see that Eoghan, our stablemaster, was in the front passenger seat next to George.

"Why is he coming? We're not taking the horses," I whispered as I slid in the back next to Jamie.

"I asked Eoghan to come," Mary mumbled, and I was even more surprised to see that she was blushing. "We need help carrying the bags."

I refrained from pointing out that we'd always done fine with just George. I leaned back, closing my eyes against the rattling and sputtering of the motor, which was protesting the watered-down fuel. George had been adding corn oil to the petrol to make it last longer. Bella jumped in beside me and I patted her soft dark fur.

"Wait!" I heard a tapping and opened my eyes to see Polly running alongside the truck, waving at me. I quickly rolled down the window, and she tossed a white envelope into my lap.

"I almost forgot," she gasped, "to give this to you."

I clutched it tight to my chest. "I'll read it on the train! Good-bye, Polly!" I turned and waved out the back of the Jeep, watching her figure grow smaller and smaller until she disappeared in the mist.

4

AFTER THE SEVENTEEN DAYS, MY FATHER HAD AN OLD VICTORIAN steam train taken out of the underground tunnels, where it had been used as a museum piece. We visited it once when I was very little: I remembered chasing Mary around the red velvet seats, drinking tea in the dark-paneled dining carriage. Now, as the only train in the country that ran on coal, it was also the only train able to run at all. A few coaches were kept open for passengers, but its main purpose was to haul heavy crates of coal, scrap metal, broken glass, wood—anything that could be melted down or welded into something usable—back to London.

We walked up to find the beautiful coaches of the old train

hidden behind reams of barbed wire fencing. Men wearing mesh masks perched on top, their guns aimed down into the crowd, holding giant three-pronged hooks so that they could pry off any stowaways. Crowds of people shoved and pushed on the platform; some had tickets, while others tried to barter cans of food, dried meat, even clothes and mittens for a seat.

"Ticket holders only!" the conductor shouted at the crowd. "Stowaways will be thrown off on sight!" I held tight to Jamie's hand as George and Eoghan rushed us through the crowd to the Royal Compartment.

We were quiet as the train pulled out of the station. Jamie drew stick figures in the misted glass of the window, then wiped them away with his sleeve. Bella curled up on her blanket by my feet. I looked out at the abandoned towns we were passing. The setting sun cast eerie shadows on an old playground. The chains had been cut from the rusted swing sets, probably to be made into weapons, or to be used by the Roamers to tie up their captives. I shuddered, thinking of how close to danger Jamie and I had come.

Eventually, the moon appeared in the sky, but even the moon was different after the Seventeen Days. It was a grayish color, and splotchy, as though it too was covered in the fine gray ash that had fallen over everything. Jamie had once asked me if the moon was sick, just like him.

The cabin grew dark. Mary reached for the coal-light, compressed coal ash inside a heat-resistant glass bulb. Slowly the black mound turned blue, then red, casting a circle of golden light above us. She pulled out two ball gowns and a sewing kit from her case. Jamie fished out a book of crosswords and a packet of colored pencils, and started drawing pictures of colorful, fiery trains. I looked at the gowns spilling over Mary's knees. One was the color of wine, with crystal beading sewn around the neckline, while the other was a simple peach-colored silk gown with a ruffle along the sleeves.

"Which one are you going to wear?" I asked, realizing that I hadn't even thought about tomorrow night's ball.

"The red one. I'm mending this one for you. It will be perfect with your eyes."

"Thank you, Mary," I said softly.

"It was Mum's, so it'll look good on you."

I said nothing, just watched the careful movement of Mary's needle along the seam. Once upon a time we had a whole staff of royal seamstresses, but Mary had learned to do a lot since the Seventeen Days. "I found them in the storage wardrobe. Remember how she used to let us play dress-up in there? This was the dress she was wearing the night she met Dad."

I thought of the room in Buckingham Palace filled with dresses belonging to past princesses and queens. The magnificent white wedding gowns worn by Princess Diana and Princess Kate, the fur-lined cloak Queen Elizabeth wore the day of her coronation. But I couldn't remember the story behind the peach dress.

I made myself smile, but inside I ached. Mary had so much more of our mother than I would ever have, and Jamie, none at all.

He looked up from his notebook, his wide blue eyes shifting anxiously from Mary to me. "Do you think Dad will be happy to see us?"

"Of course he will," Mary scolded. "Why would you even ask that?"

Jamie shrugged. "Because he never came this summer. He's been gone since June."

Mary gently brushed his hair away from his forehead. "He's been very busy with work this summer. He had to meet with the prime minister almost every day," she explained.

"Did he ever say why exactly?" I asked.

Mary shook her head, but I had the feeling she knew more than she was saying. "The rebuilding projects, I guess." Strands of her thick blonde hair fell loose from her ponytail and down the shoulders of her cream-colored blouse. Our mother always said Mary had roses in her cheeks, but I couldn't help noticing how very pale she looked these days.

Silence fell as we ate the sandwiches Clara had packed for us and shared the jar of well water. It tasted cool and fresh. Like the gasoline, the well was guarded day and night. Clean water was so hard to find now, a treasured commodity.

I turned to the train window as we passed through the outskirts of an abandoned coastal city called Callington. The buildings had collapsed like a pile of toy blocks. Pieces of debris floated like dead flies on the water. A peeling, faded billboard was scrawled in black paint with the words THE NEW GUARD IS RISING.

I shivered at the menacing words, uncertain what they meant. "Mary, what is that?" I asked.

"What, Eliza?" But by the time she turned to look, we had already passed it.

The train rocked rhythmically over the rails and soon Jamie lay asleep between us. I covered him with the blanket and tucked it under his chin.

"He looks so peaceful when he sleeps," I whispered.

Mary nodded, placing her hand on his cheek. "It's the only time he's not in pain."

I held my breath. I wondered if she suspected what had happened this afternoon. I wanted so badly to tell her, but she had enough to worry about.

"I'm getting sleepy too." Mary unfolded another plaid woolen blanket and covered herself with it. I turned down the coal lamp and laid my head on the pillow.

"Eliza?" Mary whispered, and my heart skipped a beat. I was certain she would ask me about what happened. "Do you think the red dress is too dark for my skin?"

I stared up at the dark ceiling, fighting a strange urge to laugh. Why were we holding a ball while bands of criminals stalked our lands? Roses didn't even grow anymore. But I knew that the Roses Ball was one last thread of tradition that Parliament could cling to. Like the thread in Mary's needle, desperately trying to repair the holes.

"Mary, you know you'd look beautiful in a potato sack."

I was about to close my eyes when a burst of orange flame came cascading through the sky, leaving smaller trails of fire in its wake. I sat up, watching it anxiously to see where it would land. A flash of heat passed the train window, then disappeared in an instant. The sky went black again. The sunball had died out falling to earth.

The flare was gone, but I couldn't bear to take my eyes from the dark fields. I watched, waited, just in case another one fell from the sky. The sunballs—pieces of the sun that spun off toward Earth—had been falling out of the sky since the Seventeen Days. No one knew exactly what caused them, but getting caught in their fiery rain was fatal.

Even after the destruction of the Seventeen Days, we had been hopeful. There was still electricity thanks to the backup generators, which my father allotted for use in the hospitals and fire and police stations. The hum of the generators was oddly comforting—it was the sound of rebuilding, of putting the pieces back together. The water lines were destroyed, the sun was hidden behind a cloud of ash, but as long as I heard the generators, I hoped everything would somehow be okay.

Except that England was utterly alone.

My father had sent the *Queen Mary*, the navy's eight-thousand-ton steel warship, to find news of the rest of the world. The earth had stilled, laying itself down among the mess like an exhausted child after a temper tantrum, but the oceans were still furious. The *Queen Mary* only made it a few miles offshore before the ocean swallowed her whole. There wasn't enough fuel to send another ship, and no one had answered a single one of our radio transmissions. Maybe we were the only survivors.

I pressed my hand against the window glass, still warm from the burst of the sunball's flame. The cabin suddenly felt unbearably cold. I shrugged into my coat, putting my hands in the pockets, and felt the sharp corner of an envelope. I'd forgotten about Polly's letter. I unfolded it with a smile and started to read.

Dear Eliza,

I am so sorry to have to tell you this. You are my best friend and if anything happened to you I would never feel whole again.

Do you remember my uncle, the one who worked in a metal factory before the electricity stopped? Late last night he banged on our door with his wife and their baby son. They said they had been lucky enough to escape a raid on the district LS12 in Manchester, a raid led by a group calling themselves the New Guard. They had weapons, guns, and ammunition, and they were shooting everyone who resisted. My uncle's family was able to escape through the underground to another district. They were the lucky ones.

My uncle said the New Guard have already seized many of the districts in London. They are led by Cornelius Hollister, who wants to kill your entire family and become king.

Please be careful, Eliza. Your life is in danger.

Polly

My hands trembled as I held the letter. In the dim glow of the coal lamp, I looked at my brother and sister sleeping soundly.

It dawned on me that all summer I had not heard any news of the outside world. Usually the Carriers brought us updates from London when they delivered letters from our father, but this year Clara had collected the mail for us. I thought of the time I walked into the kitchen and saw her with her ear pressed to the radio. She had switched it off as soon as she saw me, claiming that all she could find was static.

I sank back into the train's seat, staring out at the dark night. I wondered how much my father knew of Cornelius Hollister's plan and how much he was trying to hide from us. Maybe that was the reason he had stayed in London all summer.

As the light started to break through the fog, London came into view: the beautiful spires of Westminster Abbey; the sharp, glinting Steel Tower, the maximum-security prison, rising above it all; the London Eye still against the skyline, frozen, like the hands of Big Ben. When the disasters of the Seventeen Days hit London six years ago, the clock had stopped at eleven fifteen, and it was never set right again. To me the clock appeared normal, just as it had always been. But as the train charged into the city, I considered how little I understood of anything at all.

5

WE FOLLOWED THE GUARDS THROUGH PADDINGTON STATION IN the predawn darkness, dodging the shafts of cold rain that poured through the broken ceiling. Past the boarded-up ticket windows, past the workers unloading freight cars of coal and wood, past the white-haired woman in the deserted food court, selling cups of tea from an aluminum pot. The dust falling from the ceiling settled on our heads like snow.

Outside the station, the morning air was already thick with gray soot. The street felt eerily deserted. Without artificial light it was impossible for anyone to begin work until later in the morning. Our black Aston Martin was the only car on the street, though there were plenty of horses, most tethered to wagons or crude-looking carts. A few wealthier citizens who could afford to keep a pair of horses had chained them by their saddles to salvaged metal trucks. They looked awful, with wide, sad eyes and thin bodies. I thought of Jasper, well fed and free to run through the fields of Scotland, and felt guilty.

"The drains are overflowing," Mary complained as she stepped into the car.

I could only nod as we pulled out and headed toward the palace. I clutched Polly's letter in my pocket. Flooded streets were the least of our problems.

As we entered the gates of Buckingham Palace, the guards stood to attention, saluting us, still wearing their traditional black hats and red coats with shiny brass buttons. The palace itself hadn't really changed, though the brick-and-limestone facade was darkened from the dirty air and most of the windows had been boarded up to keep out the cold. We lived in a small section of the palace, closing off the rest to conserve light and precious heat. There was so little oil left in our tanks that we saved it for the coldest days.

Inside the great hall of the East Wing, our father stood

waiting for us, flanked by two guards holding swords. As excited as I was to see him, I stopped when I saw the guards. They had never been there before.

"Mary, Eliza, Jamie!" our father called out in his booming voice, holding out his arms. I ran to him, burying my face in his soft sweater, breathing in his familiar spicy scent. I wanted to stay in his arms, to fall asleep there and never leave, but instead I pulled back and felt for the letter in my pocket. "Dad," I said quietly. "I need to talk to you alone."

"Alone?"

"Yes," I whispered in his ear. "Polly says—"

"Eliza," my father stopped me, his voice terse. "This is not the time."

He turned away from me to address Mary and Jamie in an overly happy voice. "Tell me everything about your summer! Did you swim? Ride? Did the blackberries grow this year?" He lifted Jamie in the air like an airplane as the sound of my brother's laughter filled the hall. It was the first time I had heard him really laugh since we had left for Balmoral three months ago.

But all too soon his laughter turned into a deep, rasping cough. My father hugged Jamie, patting his back.

"I'm okay, Dad," Jamie managed, trying to hold back the next coughing fit.

"We're getting you some medicine right now." My father carried Jamie down the corridor toward the palace doctor, not even looking back at me and Mary. The brittle sound of our brother's cough echoed through the hall after them.

I reached out and took Mary's hand in mine, forcing a smile and shoving the letter deep in my pocket.

"Let's go to the ballroom," I said, "and help decorate for tonight and try on our dresses. I'll let you do my hair and makeup however you want." I hated getting dressed up, and Mary knew it. She smiled through her tears and squeezed my hand in response.

"Let's go the fun way," she said, and we laughed as we kicked off our shoes, racing down the palace hallways, sliding in our socks on the cold marble floors.

The ballroom had always been my favorite of all the rooms in the palace—especially the hand-painted ceiling, with its angels and fluffy clouds and shiny silver stars. When I was little I used to bring my blanket and pillow down there at night and just lie on the floor, staring up at it. I liked to imagine I was floating in the clouds, flying from star to star. After my mother died, I started to imagine it was Heaven and that I could come here to visit her.

Balls had always been Mary's specialty, but I did have a secret weakness for the Roses Ball. In the time before the Seventeen Days, on the day of the Roses Ball, we had fresh red and white roses delivered to the palace in great wooden cartons, hundreds and hundreds of roses, so many that the scent of them filled the whole palace and spilled out into the surrounding streets. But in the years since, we had to make do with brittle preserved roses. They had no scent and were the color of dried blood, not the fresh red color of living petals. Father and Mary insisted on them for tradition's sake, but they were so ugly they made me want to cry. I would rather have no roses at all than these horrible dead things.

Mary and I walked inside the ballroom, and I noticed with relief that the roses hadn't been brought up from the cellars yet.

Two maids, Margaret and Lucille, came toward us wearing their black-and-white uniforms. "Hello, Princess Mary, Princess Eliza. Welcome home," they said as we gave them each a hug.

"It looks beautiful!" Mary skipped onto the dance floor, twirling in her socks, her arms spread out like wings. "We want to help. What can we do?"

Margaret took a long handwritten list from her apron

pocket. In the past no one would have let us even *see* the ball-room in its preparatory stages, much less accept our help. But Margaret nodded and said, "Well, for starters, the silver needs polishing and the napkins need folding."

I looked up to where Rupert, our butler, stood on a high ladder, lighting each of the white candles in the enormous crystal chandelier hanging from the center of the ceiling. It had crashed to the floor during the Seventeen Days and many of the crystals were shattered, but when it was all lit up, you almost couldn't tell.

I looked down at the silver on the table and started polishing, while the rain danced on the frosted glass windows.

"Princesses! To what do I owe the pleasure of your company?" our father teased when Mary and I walked into the dining room an hour later. He stood at the head of our massive twelve-foot dining table, raising a glass of red wine. "I'm so glad you're able to join our celebratory lunch."

"What are we celebrating?" I asked quickly. My heart started to race. Had Cornelius Hollister been captured?

My father looked baffled, his glass in the air. "We're celebrating being together again as a family."

I nodded and slipped my hand in my pocket, gripping

the letter, while my father drank the glass of red wine in one long sip.

"Eliza, sweetheart. Aren't you going to join us?"

I glanced at Mary and Jamie, then down at the table, which had been set with my favorite china, each piece hand-painted with a different bird in red, gold, and yellow. A platter in the center contained brown bread and sliced cheese, a small pat of butter, and four bowls of broth with vegetables. The food looked delicious, but I knew I wouldn't be able to take a bite until I showed him the letter.

"No," I said, hearing my voice shake. I rarely spoke up to him and even more rarely disobeyed him. He was my father, but he was also the king of England. "Dad, this is important."

He grunted in anger, throwing his napkin down on the table as he pushed his chair back and walked toward me. I stepped into the hallway, out of earshot of the dining room.

"What's this all about?" he asked roughly. Beads of sweat formed on his forehead and he wiped them away with his sleeve. I handed him the letter and watched as he read it, fury evident on his face.

"Well, is it true?" I asked, unable to conceal the impatience in my voice.

He folded the letter, following the creases that were already there. "Polly has always had a wild imagination," he said dismissively. "Remember how she used to get you to spend hours in the woods waiting for goblins and flower fairies? Now come, the soup is getting cold."

I reached for his hand, grabbing his sleeve to stop him. "You didn't answer my question. Is there any truth to what Polly wrote?"

"Eliza," he began, his voice low and measured. He glanced over my shoulder at Jamie and Mary at the other end of the dining room, too far away to overhear. "Let's not talk about this now. Let's enjoy being together again as a family."

"Dad! Please. I want to know."

"There have been a few reported sightings of Cornelius Hollister, yes. But there is nothing to fear." He placed his hand reassuringly on my shoulder. "We are well protected. There is no way he will ever touch our family again."

"But—"

"Enough of this!"

I stepped quickly out of the way as he stormed by. Mary and Jamie looked up from the other side of the room. "Now, come and join us for lunch," he ordered, pulling my chair out from beneath the table.

I stared down at the floor. A mixture of shame and anger caused my chin to quiver.

I lifted my gaze from the rug. "I'm not hungry," I

announced, turning away. I felt my eyes fill with tears as I ran down the hallway, too proud to turn back now. I ran and ran until I reached my bedroom, where I pulled the curtains closed and curled up on my bed. Only then did I finally let myself cry. I cried for the summer without our father, for the awful note Jamie had left in his diary, for Polly's family, for my family, for all the suffering and destruction. I cried until I finally fell asleep from exhaustion.

A knocking sound awoke me. "Eliza?" Mary came and sat next to me on the bed. "I brought you this." She placed a plate of food on my lap. "The ball is in an hour. You need to eat something and get dressed."

Mary was ready, in her deep red gown with the antique lace on the hem. Her hair was pulled back in a high braided bun, a diamond tiara set atop it. She truly looked like a princess.

"Is Jamie okay?"

She shook her head slowly. "He can't come to the ball. His fever is high again and his coughing is too severe."

I felt so bad for Jamie; he would miss out on another piece of his life, alone in his room while the party went on below him.

"I know you're angry with Dad. But please try to make

this a nice event. I left your dress hanging in your closet."
Mary turned to go.

"Wait—" I asked, and she stopped in the doorway. "Will
you help me get ready?"

6

THE ORCHESTRA PLAYED A WALTZ AS THE PROCESSION OF guests made their way through the west gallery. The state ballroom was once the largest room in all of London; even now, entering the enormous space made me feel as though I were shrinking, like Alice in Wonderland.

Mary and I descended the grand staircase to personally welcome our guests. As tradition dictated, we stood in the main hall under the gilded ceiling, greeting each guest with a smile and a polite curtsy.

Finally it was time for the Scottish reels, a tradition of the Roses Ball dating back to Queen Elizabeth I. Men were supposed to ask their secret loves to dance, like a valentine.

I sank gratefully onto the white damask settee next to the very old Lady Eleanor Blume, who had nodded off with her head on her walking stick, and watched as a handsome young man approached Mary to dance. She expertly put a hand into his open palm, and they glided off into the center of the room.

I touched the intricate embroidery on the hem of my peach-colored dress, imagining the night my parents met and thinking of their true and enduring love. I looked out at all the boys and men in the room, but I couldn't imagine falling in love with any of them.

"Now why would such a pretty girl be sitting all alone at the ball?" My father stood before me, freshly shaven with his dark hair combed back. "May I have this dance, my darling Eliza?"

I glanced up at him. "I'm still mad at you."

"I'm sorry," he said. "I should have explained what was really going on earlier in the summer. But what I said is true. I will *never* let anyone hurt this family again." He held my gaze, his arm outstretched. "So may I have this dance?"

"Dad," I sighed. "You know I'm terrible at Scottish reels. My feet get all muddled up."

"I'm the king of England, and I command you to stand on my feet," he replied, winking.

I groaned, but stood up and took my father's hand in mine. I placed one foot on each of his shiny black shoes.

"You're heavier than I remembered," he teased.

"This was your idea." I rested my head against his chest and closed my eyes as he struggled to move his feet beneath my weight. Finally I laughed and stepped off, my shoes touching the wooden floor as I followed his footsteps.

My father twirled me out, then in again, making the room spin dizzily. The other dancers twirled around us, ball gowns of all colors—red, green, gold—swirling like a flock of exotic birds. I thought of the parties we used to have at the palace when my mother was still alive. Mary and I would hide behind the potted plants, sneaking desserts and whispering about whose dress was the most beautiful. If we had been watching this night, I thought, admiring the way Mary's crushed velvet dress brought out the color in her lips and cheeks, she would have won.

Suddenly, a shard of glass fell from the window to the floor. Then another, and another—a symphony of broken glass exploding in the air. The music stopped, and the dancers froze. My father grabbed my hand as we stared in stunned silence at the broken windows above. It seemed at first like a fantastic party trick, the shattered pieces sparkling like diamonds as they fell.

Then there was panic and screaming. The ballroom floor was covered in shards of glass, some of them glistening wetly with blood. I knew that my arm had been cut, but I ignored it. "Mary!" I cried, pushing my way through the chaos.

The palace guards charged in on horseback, and I breathed a sigh of relief. But as they began overturning tables and chairs, and lighting the curtains on fire, I realized with a jolt that they were not the guards who had protected me my entire life. They were impostors.

"Mary!" I shouted again, but the room was full of screams and my cries went unheard.

My father pushed me back to the wall. "Stay here," he told me firmly.

The men on horseback stampeded toward him from across the room, knocking down everyone in their path. An elderly lady moaned on the floor of the ballroom, her white hair stained with blood from a gash on her temple. I watched in terror as my father stood in front of one of the charging horses, trying to grab the reins from the rider before he trampled the old woman to death.

"Why are you doing this?" I screamed into the room.

A guard turned his horse on me suddenly, backing me up against the wall. "What did you say?"

I looked up into a pair of cold blue eyes. I recognized him

instantly. The bright blond hair, the gleaming white teeth—this was the face that haunted my nightmares. The man who had killed my mother. Cornelius Hollister.

He had been watching us. Waiting. Somehow my anger overpowered my fear. If he was going to kill me, I wanted him to at least answer me first.

"Why are you doing this to us?" I repeated, loudly and yet more calmly this time.

He turned, looking back at his army as though searching for an answer. "Because you represent an era that must come to an end. Because while England starves, you are having a *ball*." He dismounted. I willed myself not to back away as he stepped closer. He pulled his gun and held it to my chest.

The cold metal pressed against the silk of my dress. I didn't dare take my eyes off him. All it would take was one move of his index finger, and I would be dead.

"I'm sorry, Princess Eliza," he said, not sounding sorry at all as he clicked back the hammer on his pistol. I closed my eyes, body tensed, hands in tight fists, and waited for him to shoot.

"Put the gun down now." It was my father's voice. He stood utterly still, aiming a golden, pencil-thin revolver at Cornelius Hollister. Without warning, he pulled the trigger.

As if in slow motion, the bullet hit Hollister's vest, making a pinging sound as it fell to the floor. I stared in confusion at the useless bullet, lying there like a lost penny. Hollister was unharmed. In that moment of distraction, my father ran to me. I felt for one last, brief moment the safety of his arms. Then Hollister looked up, his cold blue eyes narrowed to angry slits.

"No!" I screamed as he pulled the trigger. The bullet entered through my father's back and exited through his chest. He fell to the floor, his body going limp.

"Dad!" I cried, pressing my hands helplessly against the flower of blood already staining his white tuxedo shirt.

"I-I'm so sorry," he murmured, his voice trembling. He tried to reach for me, but his hand dropped to his side and his body went still. I knew in that moment my father was gone.

Everything around me, the chaos, the noise, the fighting, all fell away as I stared at him in numb disbelief. A pair of hands was gripping my shoulders, pulling me up, away from him, and I tried to shake them off.

"Eliza! Come on!" Mary's voice awoke me from my trance. She deftly wove a path through the confusion, pulling me to the hidden servant's doorway beneath the back stairs.

As we ran for our lives through the hail of bullets flying around the ballroom, I risked glancing backward one last time. The body of our father lay still, his blood as red as the roses strewn across the floor.

7

MARY FUMBLED WITH THE LATCH TO THE SERVANTS' STAIR, HER hands shaking. I covered my ears, trying to block out the screams, the sound of gunfire, the crashing of horses' hooves. Finally she yanked the door open and rushed inside, pulling me sharply behind her.

I followed her up the narrow stair, clutching my gown so I wouldn't trip. Mary moved with purpose, her quick, sure steps conveying what I refused to face: She was now the queen of England.

At the top of the stairs we came to a long corridor with Persian rugs and dark wooden moldings, where a row of shaded candles illuminated our way. Somewhere in the great maze of halls I imagined I could hear Hollister's army approaching.

On a door up ahead, a string of rainbow-colored blocks spelled out JAMIE'S ROOM. I tore the sign from the door, the thread breaking in my hand, the blocks tumbling to the ground. I had helped Jamie make the sign when he was four years old. I remembered sitting together in front of the fire, drinking hot chocolate with honey as we strung the blocks together. Even though it was after the Seventeen Days, that memory suddenly felt like it was from a different time—so long ago that it was impossible to reach.

Mary swept past me and pushed open the door. The room was quiet, the pale blue curtains fluttering in the wind. In the dim light, Mary and I rushed over to Jamie's bed. The covers were pushed back, the bed empty. All that remained was his beloved Paddington Bear.

"They've taken him." Mary's voice shook with panic. I stared in disbelief at the empty bed. Mary reached for the bear with the missing eye.

I willed myself to feel something. Even crying would have been a relief.

"What's wrong?"

Through the waves of my sorrow, I must have imagined my brother's voice. I lifted my head. In the hazy light I saw

Jamie standing in front of me, wearing his blue-and-white-striped pajamas, his hair messy from sleep.

"Jamie?" My voice broke as I said his name. "Is that you?"

"Who else would it be?"

"Jamie!" Mary exclaimed, tears running down her cheeks. "Where have you been? You weren't in your bed. We thought . . ." She sounded as though she were scolding him, and Jamie stepped back in fear.

"I fell asleep on the window seat," he started to explain.

"Oh, Jamie, something terrible has happened." Mary reached out to him, and he ran forward to hug us both. He smelled of children's shampoo and cough medicine.

The sound of heavy footsteps echoed in the hallway outside.

"What's happening?" Jamie looked fearfully from Mary to me.

"Shush." Mary put her fingers to her lips. Shadows moved across the strip of light under the bedroom door.

"They're right outside," I whispered. I took Jamie's chair from beneath his desk and wedged it firmly under the door handle. I knew it wouldn't be enough to stop them, but at least it would slow them down.

"Mary?" Jamie looked at our sister, his eyes flashing with fear.

"We'll explain everything later," I answered, surprised at how calm I sounded. "Right now we have to find a way out." I made a quick mental survey of the room. Fierce red flames danced outside the window, curling inward like hands trying to grab at us. I tried to see through the blaze to the courtyard below, where the real royal guards were fighting the impostors. Bullets and spears flew through the air. The bodies of dead soldiers littered the cobblestones.

Without warning, an axe blade smashed at the door. The chair I had placed below the handle broke into tiny pieces that fell to the floor like toothpicks.

Mary screamed, wrapping Jamie in her arms as another axe splintered the wood. The steel blades glinted in the dim light.

"The war hutch," I whispered urgently. How had I not thought of it before?

Jamie's eyes lit up. "It leads to the underground tunnels. We can escape that way!" The ancient passage hadn't been used since the Second World War.

Mary grabbed the bedspread and an armful of Jamie's sweaters. We ducked into Jamie's closet and moved toward the back wall, moving our hands over the wood in the darkness, searching for the hidden latch.

"I found it!" Jamie cried out excitedly. Even through my fear, I felt a swell of pride.

The hidden door slid open to reveal a small pulley elevator, a dumbwaiter designed to lower us to the safety of the tunnels below. The three of us barely fit in the compartment, sitting with our knees pressed to our chests. I reached to turn the pulley.

"My medicine," Jamie said suddenly.

My hand tightened on the ropes. Jamie wouldn't survive long without it. Mary slid open the latch and slipped out into the bedroom. I peered through the crack in the doors.

"They're not inside yet," I said, my heart racing.

Jamie hurried out after her before I could stop him. "I'll get it. I know where it is."

"Hurry. Please hurry," I whispered after them.

Just as Jamie stepped into the dark room, an enormous crash sounded. The soldiers had broken down the door. I hurried from the dumbwaiter, peering through the opening in the closet doors.

Mary held Jamie's hand and pulled him protectively behind her back. The large oak door had fallen in, knocking the lamps to the floor with a crash. Four guards marched in and grabbed them both.

Mary kicked and hit, fighting off the guards with every

ounce of her strength. But then another one grabbed Jamie, shoving him to the ground and pressing a sword to his throat. Mary stopped resisting. She risked a single, meaningful glance over her shoulder, as though willing me to understand, before turning carefully back to the guards.

I knew what she meant—she wanted me to escape. I looked at the dumbwaiter. If I stayed, I would be taken captive with them. But how could I leave?

"Where's the other one?" the guard who seemed to be in charge yelled at Mary. She stood there silently, biting her lip. "Answer me!" When she still said nothing, he raised his fist, hitting her across the face. Blood splattered from her mouth.

"Search the room," the captain ordered, directing his gaze at a guard who stood in the doorway. The younger guard began looking through Jamie's things, overturning blankets and peering under the bed. "Start with the closets," the older guard directed gruffly.

I stepped backward through the hanging clothes, crouching down in the corner. There was no time to slip back into the dumbwaiter. I scrambled around silently for something to use as a weapon, but all I could come up with was a shoe.

The younger guard opened the door and pushed aside the rows of coats and clothes, the metal hangers chiming together, the fabric swaying. Then he saw me.

He stopped, gun in hand, as we stared at each other. His dirty blond hair fell across his forehead in messy curls, and his green eyes gleamed. I sucked in my breath.

He lowered his gun and stepped backward, disappearing behind the clothes.

"It's empty," I heard him call out to the other guards. He closed the closet door, leaving me surrounded by blackness once more. "Check the back staircase."

I heard the sound of the guards hurrying from the room, their footsteps heavy in the hallways.

I sat frozen. Had he seen me or not?

I stumbled out of the closet in confusion. Jamie's bedroom was rapidly filling with black smoke. The curtains had erupted in a massive blaze. Tongues of flame shot inward on the breeze, starting small fires in the bedroom.

"Mary! Jamie!" I cried, moving through the smoke-filled room. I was still clutching one of Jamie's sweaters and held it over my mouth to protect my lungs. In just a few seconds, the flames had spread to Jamie's bed, to the carpet, to the plush cushions on the floor. Flames teased at my hair. I smothered them with a sweater, but the ends of my hair were singed.

"Mary! Jamie!" I cried again, but the only sound was the flames crackling as they engulfed the room.

They were gone, and I had no choice but to leave too.

I raced back into the closet. The air was clearer here, and I took a deep, shuddering breath as I climbed inside the dumbwaiter and pulled the lever.

When I reached the bottom, I clambered out awkwardly and set off racing down the tunnel, my feet splashing in puddles of water. It was so dark that more than once I almost ran into a wall before skidding to a frantic stop. Cobwebs broke across my face and bats fluttered around me. I smelled smoke and began to panic. The tunnels hadn't been used in more than a hundred years.

Then a tiny pinprick of light appeared in the distance, growing bigger and bigger until I realized it was a small metal rectangle. The escape hatch.

I ran to the latch and reached up, pressing my hand against the metal surface. But it was stuck, rusted shut from decades of disuse. I took a few steps backward, summoning my strength with a running start, and threw all my weight against it. The hatch broke open and I climbed out into the night.

I gasped for fresh air, but there was none. Everything was choked with smoke. I turned to look up at the palace, flames crawling like vines up its stone facade. Hollister's soldiers were swarming over the grounds, destroying everything in sight, shooting at people as they tried to flee.

I scanned the garden, looking for a way to escape. My eyes fell on the rose beds I had planted with my mother, which had been empty and barren since the Seventeen Days. A sound blasted the air like a gunshot. All glass in the palace windows was exploding outward. I ducked and covered my head with my hands as clear shards fell around me like razor-sharp hail. Then I stumbled on something and fell forward. Lying across the walkway was a small, warm pile of fur.

"Bella!" I cried, touching her chest. Her throat had been cut and her breathing was shallow and slow.

Bella looked up at me. She tried to nuzzle my hand as I stared down into her wide, brown eyes. "I'm sorry," I told her helplessly. I lay my head down on the damp ground, wrapping my arms around her. The puddle of blood spread on the stones. "I'm sorry I couldn't protect you." I felt Bella's last labored breaths and looked up at the muted stars, the smudge of moon.

I heard the heavy footsteps and harsh voices of guards searching the palace garden.

Let them catch me, I thought, *let them kill me here.* My mother was dead. My father was murdered. My brother and sister were as good as dead. They had even taken my dog from me. The weight of my sorrow fell on me heavy as a lead blanket.

I closed my eyes as I lay with Bella, waiting for them to find me and kill me too.

But instead of the cold barrel of a gun or the sharp blade of a sword, I felt a sudden softness, a wing brushing against my cheek. I touched my hand to my face, thinking I must have already died, that I was with my mother again. Then I heard a soft whistling and opened my eyes. Perched on the charred remains of the rosebush sat a small bird.

"Blue?" I whispered, still half-thinking I was imagining it.

He whistled back and then flew away into the smoke-clogged night sky.

Blue was a baby blue jay who, against all odds, had survived the Seventeen Days. Mary and I had heard his chirping and found him still alive, surrounded by the dead bodies of the other chicks, the body of their mother spread out protectively over the nest. I had picked him up, warming him in my hands—he had been so frightened, his heart beating so fast in his tiny body.

I had made a nest of straw and dug worms from the soil, crushing them and feeding them to him every few hours. I kept him safe in a box until he grew stronger. Then one day, while I was holding him, he opened his wings and flew out of the palm of my hand. He seemed so happy, almost surprised that he had wings and could fly.

I thought of Blue's joy at discovering he could fly, and something inside me made me stumble to my feet. I got up and numbly moved into the hollow of one of the last trees in the garden.

A group of soldiers rushed through the garden, passing the spot where I had been mere moments before, trampling Bella's tiny body. They carried torches, their steel-spiked boots shining in the light of the flames. At the palace entrance, another soldier opened fire on a woman running for her life, and she fell to the ground with a shuddering moan. It was Margaret, one of our maids. I screamed silently, closing my hands in fists so tight that my fingernails drew blood.

I wanted to close my eyes but refused to let myself look away. Soldiers were still looting the palace, taking weapons, food, whatever they could carry. They had even found the last remaining tanks of oil. The palace servants, the guests, everyone who hadn't been killed was being tied up and blindfolded, then loaded into the backs of canvas-covered trucks. The terrorized screams of the prisoners rose up in the night air. The soldiers ignored them and filled the tanks of the trucks with the oil they'd discovered. The words scrawled on their sides shone in the light of the dancing flames: THE NEW RULER HAS RISEN.

The trucks pulled out of the gates, the soldiers on

horseback following close behind. Then I saw him—his golden hair shining, his hand raised in victory as he rode away from the charred remains of my home.

I was alive. My life had been spared, and it could only be for one reason.

I had to kill Cornelius Hollister.

8

MY LUNGS HLHED AS I WALKED ALONG THE DESERTED HIGHWAY.

   I had lost sight of the soldiers hours ago but I kept moving steadily onward, falling forward with exhaustion. I had taken off running after the trucks outside the palace, chasing them down street after street, the taillights growing dimmer as I fell ever farther behind. Now my feet were sore, my silk dancing slippers ripped to shreds. But I had to keep going. I stayed on the road, continuing in the same direction I last saw the trucks headed. Every now and then I caught the scent of diesel and knew I was on the right track. No one had cars anymore aside from the royal family—and now, Cornelius Hollister.

I had no idea how far I walked. The Thames was my guide. Even though it reeked of brine and waste, it was oddly comforting, its familiar presence always a dark shadow on my left. I knew from its position that I was headed southwest.

I stared around me at the desolate outskirts of the city. No people to be seen, no lights on the road. A pack of rats scurried across the street and disappeared into a gutter drain. I shivered. My peach gown was little protection against the sharp winds coming off the river. I was freezing; I had lost Jamie's sweater sometime in my escape. *Jamie.* My knees buckled as I thought of the look on my younger brother's face as they took him away. But I shook my head, trying to shake the memory away. I couldn't think about last night, not yet—because when I did, when I faced the fact that my father had died and my brother and sister had been captured—I would need to grieve. And I couldn't do that right now. I couldn't stop.

The crunch of tires sounded on the road behind me. For a split second, I allowed myself to hope it was royal forces, coming to rescue me, but I knew better. There were no royal forces anymore. I jumped to the side of the road, hiding in the shadowy doorway of a boarded-up building, and hoped I wouldn't be seen.

A truck barreled past, driving down the road in the

direction I had just been walking. It was graffitied in black with the same message I had seen earlier. THE NEW GUARD IS RISING.

I started to run after it but slowed down after only a few steps. If I could follow just one of these trucks, it would take me to Cornelius Hollister's encampment. But I would never be able to keep up on foot.

The next time, I would be ready.

A flock of pigeons flew westward over the Thames. A gust of wind hit me with such force that I grabbed the steel pillar beneath the bridge, shielding my eyes from the blowing ash. Then, as suddenly as it appeared, it was gone. The air was still again.

The wind had brought in the smell of garbage, rotting and putrid. I fought the urge to hold my nose and instead headed for the riverbank. Rubbish barges used to sail down the Thames; the trash pile might have something wearable in it, and I knew I couldn't show up at the camp of the New Guard in my ball gown. I shivered as I walked along the bank. Further up I spotted the red-and-black barge, marooned below the river wall, washed ashore in one of the storms. The piles of garbage sat in stinking hills, black plastic bags torn apart. Through the dim light I saw figures moving across the piles, picking through them. They were the Collectors: the displaced and homeless, who survived only by scavenging the pitiful remains of the time before. There was less and less salvageable rubbish each year. What would happen when there was nothing left worth saving?

I had never seen the Collectors before. They only came out after nightfall.

I waited, crouching, watching them. I shivered uncontrollably in my damp, thin dress, the skin on my arms like ice, my fingers numb. I couldn't stay like this. I had no choice but to join them. I kept close to the river wall, where I could escape to the roads if I needed to, making my way carefully to the barge.

Under the mist rising from the river the Collectors scavenged the piles of rubbish. They were thin, but they seemed dangerous, as though they had been drawn with razor-sharp edges. Several of the men carried pieces of pipe, their shoulders tense, ready to strike at any moment. Pieces of garbage blew around them, and a broken plastic lawn chair tumbled in a wind gust, landing and floating in the river.

"Someone's coming," a girl exclaimed, and their heads all snapped around, their dark eyes boring into me. An older woman with tired eyes lifted her piece of pipe threateningly. I couldn't help noticing that she'd cut holes in the front of her shoes for her toes. I supposed too-small shoes were better than none at all.

"I don't want any trouble," I called out, my palms up. A girl with white-blonde hair reached behind her, pulling out an iron pole that had been sharpened at the end. She aimed it like a spear, directly at my chest.

I took a step back. "Please," I begged. "I'm just looking for clothes. For something warm."

The girl looked to a man with silver hair for approval; he nodded slowly. She lowered her spear. "Five minutes," the leader said. "This is our ground, and we don't take kindly to trespassers." They turned as one and moved away from me.

Shivering uncontrollably, I tried sifting through the plastic bags, which were wet and torn and covered in soot. Even in the cold the smell was sickening. I pulled out a broken bottle, drink cartons, plastic containers, juice boxes, a cracked and broken laptop seeping a brown liquid battery acid like blood from its silver frame. Everything was sodden, covered in mold, decaying. I stared at the piles of rubbish in defeat.

I wrapped my frozen arms around me for warmth. My hands were so cold I couldn't open or close them to look any further.

"You're shivering. Your lips are blue," I heard a voice say.

I looked up to see the blonde girl with the spear. She held something in her arms. "Here, take these." She dropped a bundle of clothes at my feet.

I tried to thank her, but my lips were too frozen to speak. Hurriedly I fumbled, pulling a woolen sweater over my head and jumping into a pair of men's trousers that fell past my feet.

"Thank you," I said, trying to form the words through numb lips. "Please, one more thing. The trucks that go by here—with the graffiti on them. Have you seen them? Do you know where they go?"

She nodded, eyeing me thoughtfully. "They come by every few hours, on the road over that wall. When you hear the trucks, hide. They'll take you if they see you. And if they take you, you never come back." She began to turn away.

"Wait!" I cried. "Please, wait." I reached my hand up to my collarbone to feel the cool touch of my locket. I had forgotten to take it off. My mother's picture and the inscription of my name, Elizabeth, would give me away instantly. I reached behind my neck to unclasp it, letting it fall into the palm of my hand, opening it for one last look at the photo of my mother. One more good-bye that I was being forced to say, long before I was ready. "Please take care of it," I said, handing it to the girl. The gold glinted in the dim light.

She looked at it in shock, as though she'd never seen anything so beautiful. Then she nodded. "Good luck." Without another word, she was running over the hills of garbage toward where the rest of the Collectors waited for her.

As I raised a hand in good-bye I heard the sound of a motor. I clambered up the wall and crouched there unsteadily, trying to make myself as small and unnoticeable as possible. The truck was approaching on my right, full of flour and food supplies. It would be an easy landing.

I held my breath, waiting until the truck was directly beneath me, and jumped.

9

I SAT IN THE BACK OF THE TRUCK, WEDGED BETWEEN A SACK OF flour and a barrel of some sloshing liquid. My heart was racing. I didn't know what kind of noise my landing had made, but the driver hadn't pulled over or even slowed down. After a few minutes, I felt safe enough to peek up and try to determine my surroundings.

Up ahead, backlit against the dark sky, was the outline of a turreted castle, the reflection of coal lights shining out of its windows. I recognized it instantly. Hampton Court.

I remembered it as the palace of Henry VIII and all his wives, a tourist destination before the Seventeen Days. Mary and I had visited many times when we were little, with our governesses Rita and Nora. We would ride on the royal river-boat, sailing through the city and out along the green banks of the countryside, waving to onlookers as we passed. It had been one of our favorite things to do in the summers. We had dressed up in white sundresses and wide-brimmed straw hats. They would close the palace to the public so we could sit in the garden for iced tea and scones.

I burrowed down under the flour sack as we passed through the front gates. Hollister's army may have needed new recruits, but I doubted they would take kindly to a stow-away on their supply truck.

The truck slowed to a stop. I waited for the driver's steps to disappear toward the entrance, but instead I heard him approaching the back of the vehicle. I sucked in my breath.

"What have we here?" A man with dirty, curly hair and a crooked nose pulled aside the sacks blocking my hiding place. He grinned at me with a mouthful of broken teeth.

"I'm here to register for the army," I said, willing my voice to sound tougher, hard and flat.

"In the back of a food services vehicle? Looks more like thievery to me."

"Please," I said quickly. "It's cold out, and I was walking all the way from London. You can check—I haven't touched a thing."

The guard eyed me strangely. I noticed his gaze moving from my face, over my chest and down to my legs. I froze. Did he recognize me?

"Well, you're in luck," he spoke quickly. "There's no registration on Sundays. Normally, you'd have to come back tomorrow morning. But since I'm a recruiting officer, I'll register you myself. It'll be our little secret."

"Thank you," I said, steadying my voice. He gestured around the corner, and I followed him along a path leading past the old gatehouse, where a sign above the doors read NEW RECRUITS.

"Is this it?" I asked, stopping in front of the door.

"After-hours registration is up this way a bit further." He pointed ahead, but all I could see was a deserted field. Suddenly I felt his arm around my shoulders.

"So what's your name, huh?"

My heart began to pound. In the palace, no one would have dared to touch me like this. But I had no idea if this was normal behavior. I smiled carefully and took a step back, slipping out from under his grasp.

"You're rather pretty," he went on, backing me up against the wall. I felt his hand against my chest and tried to squirm away.

"Please," I breathed, but he leaned in closer, pressing his mouth to mine. I screamed. "Get off me!" I reached to hit him in his torso, remembering what the Royal Master of Arms had taught us about defending yourself when stripped of your weapon, but the more I struggled, the tighter his fingers gripped my neck. I couldn't breathe. I beat at the wall, hoping someone would hear me, but my fists barely made a sound against the thick stones.

"Shut up!" he hissed, covering my mouth with his hand. I tried to kick at him, but he pressed his knee into my stomach, pinning me against the wall as he reached, fumbling, to rip open my shirt. The other hand gripped so tight around my throat I began to see spots against the back of my eyelids. I was going to pass out.

"Let her go. Now." I heard a girl's voice from what seemed like a great distance.

The hand loosened from my neck, and I gasped, taking quick, shallow breaths. Slowly my eyes began to focus. The guard stood still, his hands raised in the air, as a girl holding a sword sprinted toward us. The soldier backed away in fear.

"Hand over your sevil," she barked.

"Portia, I—"

"This is not tolerated." She lunged at him and tore off his badge. "Hand over the sevil." The guard reluctantly unhooked the weapon from his belt.

"Now leave camp or I'll castrate you myself."

"But—"

"Go!" she yelled, raising her weapon as he turned away and ran off toward the woods.

"Thank you," I said cautiously, leaning against the wall for support.

She whirled around and fixed her green eyes on me in a fierce stare. "Who are you?" she snapped.

I stammered the first name that came to mind. "P-Polly McGregor." As the words left my lips, I said a silent prayer that Polly was still safe in Scotland.

I tried to get a better look at my rescuer. She was tall and unusually beautiful, with high cheekbones and dark blonde hair falling down her back. Even though she only looked a year or so older than me, there was a steely confidence about her that made her seem much older. I wondered what position she held in the army. She seemed to outrank my attacker: Where he'd been wearing a badge, a gold medallion was pinned to her uniform. Her almond-shaped eyes looked me up and down. "You know there's no registration today."

"Yes," I mumbled, "that's what he said, and then—"

"Don't worry about him," she snapped. "He won't dare come back. If he does, I'll use him for target practice." She smiled, her teeth glinting dangerously, suggesting that she wasn't joking. "Now, where are you from, Polly McGregor?"

"Scotland."

"Scotland? Funny, you don't have a Scottish accent."

I stood up straighter. "That's because I grew up in London. I didn't move to Scotland till I was ten."

"And what are you good for exactly?" I blinked at her. "I mean," she went on, "why should I make an exception and let you register today? What skills do you have? Or will I just have to put you on latrine duty?"

"I can ride and shoot a pistol. I'm pretty good with swords, too," I added. The more access I could get to weapons, the better.

She stared at me again. I held her gaze unblinkingly. "Fine," she said finally. "You'll be in my squadron—for now—and we'll see how good you really are. I'm Portia, by the way," she added, "Sergeant, Girls' Division, Section Nine." She turned on her heel and I hurried to follow her.

"Oh, and Polly?" she added over her shoulder, not even bothering to look at me. "Don't pull a stunt like this again.

You stay out of trouble or there will be consequences. I'll see to that myself."

I nodded, not daring to speak.

"Welcome to the New Guard."

10

GIRLS' BUNK SECTION 9 WAS ON THE THIRD FLOOR, IN A LONG room with a row of tall windows overlooking the courtyard. Hampton Court's antique floors were scratched, its portraits graffitied and torn. I glanced out the window—even the gardens were destroyed, the birdbaths broken.

"This is Polly," Portia announced to the twenty or so girls in the dorm. I waited for her to make introductions, but she didn't offer. "You can have that bed," she told me, pointing to the corner. "And take this." She tossed a bulky beige laundry bag at me.

I quickly looked through the bag. It contained a uniform, brown woolen socks, and a pair of boots. No weapon. In fact,

I realized, Portia seemed to be the only one with a weapon.

I settled on my narrow metal cot and looked around the room. Most of the girls were gathered in a circle on the floor, playing a game of cards. In the pot: one silver hoop earring, a razor with a bright pink plastic handle, a bullet, a red cap with fuzzy earflaps.

On the bunk next to me sat a small Indian girl, tracing an imaginary pattern with her finger on the pea-green woolen blanket.

"I'm Polly," I said.

She looked up at me, startled. "Vashti."

"Have you been here long?"

"Not too long," she replied shyly.

Her face was delicate with big brown eyes, and her hands and fingers were so thin. "How? I mean, why did you come here?"

Her brown eyes swelled with tears and I immediately regretted asking.

"I'm sorry," I said, placing my hand on hers.

I looked over at the girls playing cards, worried they might overhear us. "Vashti," I went on quietly. "Do you know which part of the palace Cornelius Hollister lives in?"

She shook her head quickly.

"Do you know any way I can find out?"

She stared at me with her wide eyes and leaned forward to whisper in my ear. "If you don't want trouble, don't ask questions."

She turned to look at the girls, engrossed in their game, then back at me. She lifted her hair from where it fell around her neck, revealing a vicious scar. Running from her neck down her back were four bloodied, blackened lines.

I gasped. "Who did that to you?"

She lifted her chin lightly, gesturing to the girls sitting in a circle on the floor. "They did it with a fork."

I stared at the girls, imagining them pinning her to the ground, stabbing her neck with a fork and raking it through her skin. "Who *are* they?" I whispered.

"The ones you really need to watch out for—aside from Portia, of course—are June"—she gestured to a tall, pale girl wearing severe circles of dark eyeliner and swallowed nervously before continuing—"and there's Tub. She's second-in-command."

Next to Portia, at the head of the circle, sat an angry-looking brunette. Her huge, muscular arms were covered in swirls of tattoos that looked like she had carved them herself with a knife. She glared around the circle with hard, dark eyes. Just then there was a knocking on the bunk door.

"Sergeant?" an older girl asked. She wore the same

gold medallion as Portia but was clearly intimidated by her. "Lights out in ten minutes. And don't forget to put out all fires," she added timidly, eyeing the candle that flickered in the center of the card game.

"Thanks, Sarah." Portia smirked. Sarah ducked out of the doorway, and Portia clapped her hands. "You heard her, girls. Bedtime!" She swept the pile of goods toward her with a giggle, watching as everyone climbed into bed.

Once everyone was settled she walked to the doorway. "Good night, sleep tight, don't let the bedbugs bite," she said in a singsong, then blew out the candle and stepped into the hallway. The room went dark. The only dim light came from the moon, glowing weakly behind the gray clouds. The wind rattled against the tall glass windowpanes.

"Vashti," I said under my breath. "Portia doesn't sleep with us?"

"Portia? In *here*?" she whispered with a shudder, as though the thought alone terrified her. "No, she bunks with the other commanding officers on the top floor."

I rolled over to face the window, hoping to sleep, but there was a sound coming from outside. I listened harder. Underneath the gusts of wind and rattling glass, under the hushed snatches of conversation, I heard the sound of human cries.

I sat up in the dark, startled. "What's that?"

"What's what?" the girl named Tub asked.

"The screams."

"Oh, it's just the prisoners in the Death Camps," Tub said. "You'll get used to it soon enough. Now, no more talking, or I'll report you."

I stared up at the ceiling, my heart pounding in my chest as I thought of the scars down Vashti's back. *Stay calm. Don't ask questions. Be patient.* I recited the words over and over in my head, like a mantra.

I could feel the metal springs in the mattress and smelled mildew on the blanket. I turned onto my side, covering my ear with my hand. The agonizing cries echoed in my head, becoming the horrible soundtrack to the images replaying in my mind: Jamie and Mary captured by Hollister's soldiers. My father's chest soaked in blood as he lay dying on the ballroom floor. My mother hunched over, gasping, as the poisoned peach fell from her hand. The haunted, hollow faces of the Collectors by the river and the horrible yellow teeth of the soldier who had attacked me behind the gatehouse.

I gritted my teeth, burying my face in the pillow so no one would hear me cry.

When my sobs finally subsided and my breathing calmed

down, I felt oddly separated from myself, like a wall of steel was coming down, protecting the real me from the one that would now face the world.

As I felt myself drifting off to sleep, only one word echoed in my head. *Revenge.*

11

THEY WOKE US IN THE MIDDLE OF THE NIGHT. OUTSIDE THE TALL rectangles of windows the sky was inky black. I bolted upright in bed, panicked and sweating. Alarms sounded through the palace walls and the heavy rhythm of soldiers' footsteps resounded through the hallways and down the stairs, echoing against the thick stone walls. Still dazed with sleep, my eyes adjusted slowly to the darkness. I could make out the figures of the girls in the barrack dressing quickly in their uniforms.

"Hurry, get dressed," Vashti told me.

"What's going on?"

"It's the Death Night." Vashti pulled the laces on her boots tight. As she tied them in bows her hands trembled.

"Death Night?" My voice choked on the words.

She sat down beside me. "They take the prisoners they captured in the night raids and pair them up with the soldiers of the New Guard. Then we fight to the death. It's practice for battle."

In the dark, I tried to look into Vashti's brown eyes, absorbing her words. Then I heard Portia's voice calling from the doorway. "Meet outside the courtyard in ten minutes for Rank Testing."

"Hurry," Vashti said again, touching my shoulder. "You have to put your uniform on."

The night was cold and dark. I stayed close to Vashti, following the long lines of soldiers from the palace to the outside grounds. In the distance the flames of torches lit up the walled courtyard, casting flickering shadows and smoke. The flames leapt wildly in the wind, pieces of fire breaking free and dying in the air.

"To Base Court," a soldier called out, marching the lines of troops through the remains of what had once been the fountains and manicured boxwood lawns. In the light of the fiery torches, I looked up at the keep, at the guards patrolling the turret walks and the watchtower overlooking the courtyards. Under the haze of the coal lamps, guards paced up and down the grounds, patrolling.

The crowds of soldiers gathered in the courtyard, watching with excited anticipation. A diesel truck hummed at the far end, the glare of the truck's headlights casting a spotlight on the paved stone ground. The words painted in black on the truck read A NEW GUARD FOR A NEW TIME, splayed across its side like a giant banner.

A hushed silence fell over the crowd as a soldier made his way to the back of the truck. The guards parted as he pulled a masked prisoner from the back, shoving him roughly into the glare of the truck's lights.

The prisoner's hands were chained behind his back, his feet shackled, his head covered in a black cloth bag with small ovals cut out for eyes. A burly, short, red-faced guard pushed the prisoner to the center of the courtyard with the barrel of his gun.

Vashti turned to me, whispering in my ear. "That's Sergeant Fax. He's one of the cruelest guards."

"New recruits will be called at random to fight the prisoners," Portia called as she walked past the girls' division. She stood tall, stony faced, her green eyes catching the light, her sculptured, beautiful face a stark contrast to that of the terrified prisoner shivering in the courtyard. Portia's long hair was pulled back tightly in a low ponytail. A sword hung in a scabbard at her side.

"Soldier Thomas Cutter," she called out into the crowd, reading off a piece of paper.

A boy stepped forward. He looked about fifteen. His dark hair was cropped short against his scalp, the crossed sword and sevil, the symbol of the New Guard, shaved into his hairline. His brown eyes caught the light of the truck as a wide smile erupted on his face. He looked eager to fight. Portia smiled back at him and selected a weapon from a pile.

"Make it double edged," the young soldier said.

Portia pulled out a gleaming razor-thin, double-edged sword. "He's one of the Resistance forces," she informed the soldier. "Make him suffer."

The crowd of soldiers cheered him on. The noise was deafening. The masked prisoner was pushed to his knees, helplessly awaiting his opponent. Portia walked out onto the field, delivering the soldier his sword.

"Unmask him," she ordered Sergeant Fax. He pulled off the prisoner's black hood to reveal his face. He was a man in his mid-thirties, with shoulder-length brown hair and a straggly beard. His horrified eyes darted around the courtyard, a chant of "Kill him!" echoing through the square. Ragged clothes hung from his emaciated, skeleton-thin body, and open sores covered his skin.

They unchained his hands and feet as Sergeant Fax handed the man a sword, dull and unimpressive in comparison to the young soldier's. The weight of it pulled the prisoner's arms to the ground. A wild fury seemed to rage in the young soldier's eyes. He lifted his sword again, gaining momentum and strength, and brought it down on the prisoner's neck. With one desperate move, the man mustered up all of his strength and swung his sword up to block Cutter's blow.

But this only infuriated Cutter more. He stepped forward and, without giving the prisoner a moment to defend himself, plunged his long sword into the helpless man's abdomen. He let go of the pommel, leaving the sword piercing the prisoner's body. The crowd roared as the dying man stumbled backward around the courtyard, his hands wrapped around the blade, futilely trying to stanch the blood pouring from the wound.

I put my hands to my ears, trying to drown out the deafening noise of the crowd, but Portia's shrill voice cut through the din.

"New Recruit Polly. Girls' Division, Section Nine."

I stared up in shock. Vashti looked at me. I shook my head. "I can't."

"You have to," she said, squeezing my wrist. "Or they'll

send you to the work camps. Trust me. You don't want to end up there, shackled to a chain gang, beaten by the guards— they'll force you to build the death chambers."

I stepped forward, terrified. Even as the first prisoner continued to stagger to his death, Sergeant Fax pulled another masked prisoner from the back of the truck. Portia issued me my weapon, a single-edged, middle-length sword. I grabbed the leather-bound handle tightly as Sergeant Fax dragged the second prisoner toward me. All around me I heard the New Guard soldiers chanting, "Kill! Kill!"

Beneath the black mask covering his face I could see the prisoner was a man—tall, muscular, not emaciated or covered in sores like the one before. Unlike the first prisoner, now lying in a heap in front of the crowd, this man was not weak from hunger or starvation, or broken from being tortured in the Death Camps. He must have been recently captured.

On the man's wrist was a tattoo of the British flag, the words FREEDOM OR DEATH printed beneath it. I turned, looking at the darkened and blurred faces of the crowd as they shouted, "Fight! Fight!" The torches let out thick plumes of dark smoke into the night air. In the corner of the courtyard the first prisoner had finally collapsed, his fingers and eyes still twitching.

"Meet your opponent." Sergeant Fax chuckled as he pulled off the prisoner's mask.

I stared into his eyes. He stared back into mine. He had the build of a soldier, muscular and strong, his short-cropped brown hair and stubble showing signs of gray. I noticed his kind eyes.

They unchained his hands and feet. He was given a short, dull-bladed sword. We faced each other. I wondered if there was a way to let him know I was on his side, that I was here to fight the New Guard, not him. I tried to make eye contact. I stepped closer.

And then I saw his sword come down. I raised my own, stopping him with a high block, ducking with a low block. I remembered quickly what the Master of Arms had taught me: Block small, keep the sword slanted, use the whole force of your body, weight and speed behind each move.

Fierceness shone from his eyes as he slashed wildly with the sword. He wanted to destroy me. He had seen the New Guard invade his district, murder and capture his friends and family. His eyes focused on me as he raised his sword and charged. I backed up, blocking his swings, our swords clashing deafeningly, the weight of his blows pushing me backward.

I blocked as swiftly as I could, but the sword kept flashing toward me in a blur of steel. Without warning, his blade slashed through my shoulder, cutting the fine mesh of my uniform but not piercing my skin. Before I turned my eyes from the gash his sword grazed my knuckles like a thousand needling paper cuts. Blood trickled down my wrist. It was all I could do to grasp the pommel handle and not let it fall to the ground. I felt the warm blood dripping down my arm. From the corner of my eye I saw Sergeant Fax watching grimly.

I remembered a trick the Master of Arms taught us: telegraphing. I looked to the right. He raised his sword to block. But instead of raising my sword, I slashed from beneath. He screamed out in anger and pain, looking down at his wrist. A gash of blood appeared where my sword had broken his skin. I parried his lead hand with my sword, stepping behind him. He turned his head sharply, but before he could block me, I brought the blade to his neck.

If he moved even one millimeter now, the razor-sharp sword would slice through his throat. The prisoner gasped. I could feel his body trembling with fear as sweat beaded on his forehead and soaked his clothes. I couldn't help but look at his tattoo, the British flag glistening beneath dribbles of his blood.

"Cut his head off!" a soldier screamed from the side, and then came the loud chant of the others, overlapping until they found their rhythm. "Slit his throat! Make him bleed!"

I held the sword at his neck. Hidden in the roar of the soldiers, I whispered in his ear, "You fought for the Resistance?"

"Yes, and I'll fight to my death."

He turned to take a swing at me, my sword grazing his skin.

I pressed closer. "Drop your weapon now and I won't kill you."

He tilted his head skeptically, but without any other option, he let the sword fall from his hand to the pavement. Still keeping my sword at his neck, I reached to grab his weapon. I'd won. I stepped back away from him with both weapons in my hands. I thought the crowd would cheer for me, but they were silent. I looked around the courtyard. The soldiers stared back at me.

Sergeant Fax appeared on the field. "Finish him!" he ordered.

I looked from the eyes of the soldier to Sergeant Fax. Before I could refuse, Sergeant Fax grabbed the soldier's hair in one hand, my wrist and sword in the other, and forced my arm to swing. The force of the blow severed the prisoner's arteries, and blood poured from his neck in a deluge. I stumbled backward, frantically trying to wipe his blood from my eyes. All I saw was red.

"If you hesitate on the battlefield, you'll be killed," Sergeant Fax screamed into my face. Then, seeing the tattoo of the British flag on the prisoner's right arm, he took his own sword, stepping on the prisoner's elbow with his heavy black boot, and sawed off the tattooed wrist. I tried not to look at the dismembered hand on the concrete. Sergeant Fax stabbed it through the palm with the tip of his sword, raising it in the air as the soldiers cheered.

12

I STUMBLED BACK TO THE SIDELINES, FRESH BLOOD DRIPPING
from the blade of my sword. Grotesque images flashed
through my mind, and I pressed my hand to my mouth. I
could see the blood spurting from his wound. I could feel
Sergeant Fax's hand over mine, guiding the sword through
the prisoner's neck, the give of flesh as the blade slashed
through the delicate skin.

The crowds were already cheering on the next fight,
too distracted to notice me. I shoved my way through them
blindly, my hands trembling.

I stumbled into an empty courtyard surrounded by a
cloistered passageway. Carved statues of lions and ravens and

horses, gargoyles and dragons, lined the walls. The metallic taste of the prisoner's blood coated my mouth. I retched, struggling to vomit, but there was nothing in my stomach.

My eyes closed. I collapsed to the ground, hugging my knees to my chest and shaking uncontrollably. I had ended an innocent life. Across the dark courtyard, I saw a crumbling stone birdbath running over with rainwater. I pushed myself up, walking out of the cloistered walkway. The inky darkness of the night sky was slowly giving way to another gray morning. I made my way over to the bath and dropped my sword, cupping my hands in the ice-cold rainwater to rinse the blood from my eyes and mouth. The water fell from my hands in pink streams.

I stared up at the massive redbrick walls surrounding me and scanned the remains of the crumbling statues in the garden when I realized that I was alone. I was alone, and I had a deathly weapon. I dipped the blade in the water, watching the blood dissipate. I hated Cornelius Hollister and his army beyond all conceivable feelings or fear I had for my own life. Now that I was truly a killer, it was time for me to find the man I'd come here to kill.

I took in the vast palace compound. Lights shone from the top floor of the tower keep. Legions of troops patrolled the fortress. I stared up at the lighted windows. Could Cornelius

Hollister be living there? In the keep, he would be protected, but could still watch over his army. Of everywhere in London, being stationed within his army compound made the most sense, and within the compound, only the keep would ensure his safety. But it would not be easy to get inside.

I crept through the cloisters, stepping softly and stopping every couple of feet to listen to my surroundings. I held the sword at the ready as I hurried through the cloister archways.

Suddenly, a blaring noise echoed through the palace, soldiers screaming out into the night. I recognized Sergeant Fax's voice sounding through a bullhorn. "Three prisoners have escaped the Base Court. Send all troops to the gateway. Repeat. Three prisoners have escaped. Two soldiers have been wounded. Secure all gateways immediately." I quickly ducked behind a pillar and waited in the shadows, barely breathing, frozen in my steps.

Following the orders, the soldiers took off, some on horseback, some on foot, searching the grounds. I peered around the pillar, watching the soldiers, guns in hand. Their heavy black steel-toed boots stomped the ground, echoing through the courtyard as they tore past me.

To my left, the ironclad doors of the keep stood open. A single young guard remained outside, left alone, as the others searched for the escaped prisoners. His pale face was lit by the flames of the torch. He was young, fourteen maybe, and he gripped his rifle close to him, pacing nervously.

I felt the ground, looking for something to throw. My fingers found a piece of brick that had fallen from the palace walls. Hiding in the narrow alcove of a barred casement window, I hurled the brick into the darkness, aiming it to the far right of the soldier.

The sound startled the boy. He raised his gun. "Who's there?" His voice shook with fear.

I found a second brick and threw it further past the boy. He hesitated before aiming his gun into the empty darkness, then took a few steps forward, away from the entrance.

"Who's there?" he called again into the darkness.

I bolted from my hiding place, sprinting through the wide iron doorway, and found myself inside a cavernous room filled with metal cargo containers. I ducked between them, waiting to see if I'd been spotted. As my eyes adjusted to the dim glow of light streaming down from the upper floors, I realized I was inside a storage facility. The spray-painted labels on the sides of the metal cargo bins read ZYKLON B, CYANIDE, HCN. A strong smell of gasoline came from two metal holding tanks. Wooden crates labeled with number codes held dismantled army Jeeps and trucks, generators side by side with old-fashioned weaponry. Bomb-cannons, fire-arrows, shields, armor, and swords were all stockpiled inside.

Wedging myself between the crates, I sidestepped to the cargo bin labeled FIREARMS. I tried to lift it, hoping I'd find a gun, but the box was locked and the sides were welded shut. I heard a humming sound coming from above and I looked up, startled. It was the murmuring of voices. I felt my heart beating rapidly as I hurried up the stairs and crouched down to hide in the dark landing.

I followed the sound of the voices down the passageway until I saw a ribbon of fluorescent light spilling from a door-way. I pressed my back to the wall, pulling my sword from its sheath as I crept forward. Inside the cavernous chamber, the generals of Hollister's army sat around a long, heavy oak table, their backs to the door. Blueprints, maps, and diagrams covered the walls.

"The plans to build camps F through J are set to begin in Field Eleven." A younger soldier stood at the front of the room, pointing to the diagrams. "We have a location for the royal crown. One of the tortured Royalists confessed." I chanced a look into the room, scanning the ranks of the New Guard for Hollister's face.

"I knew we'd find our answer with the enhanced interro-gation techniques," a second soldier, a woman, said.

"*Extraordinarily* enhanced interrogation techniques," another voice said, laughing.

I pressed my back to the wall. A light flickered on the floor above. To get there I would have to pass the doorway. Peering into the room from the corner of my eye, I waited until the soldier had his back turned, then shot past the doorway as quickly as possible. The sound of metal on metal reverberated through the hallway as the blade of my sword struck the stairway railing. I froze. A wave of cold fear swept over me.

"Who's there?" The soldier who'd been addressing the room appeared in the doorway. "What are you doing here? No unauthorized officers allowed in the keep." His voice was firm, angry.

I shook my head, unable to speak.

"Answer me!" he ordered.

Desperately I tried to think of an excuse. "I'm sorry. I'm lost, I was just trying to find my bunk." Frightened, I stepped away from him, out of the light, keeping my eyes low. I glanced up at his face, and our eyes caught. In that instant I recognized him. Dark blond hair, deep-set green eyes, high cheekbones. He was the guard who had left me in the wardrobe during the invasion of Buckingham Palace.

"You got lost in the keep?" He stared at me suspiciously. Did he recognize me too? The last time he saw me, I was wearing makeup and a beautiful ball gown. Now my hair and face were dirty, and I wore the uniform of his army. This was the last place he should expect to find me. For all he knew, I had been burnt to ashes in Buckingham Palace.

"Yes. It's my first day here," I stammered, not concealing the fear in my voice. If he could tell how afraid I was, maybe he would believe I really was a hopelessly lost new recruit.

He took another step closer. I looked back at him through wide eyes and gripped my hands in tight fists to stop them from trembling. Fear lurched in my stomach. Should I try to run? I glanced behind me, gauging the distance from the banister railing to the floor below. I could jump. But landing on the stones might break my ankles, maybe even my legs.

"This time it's a warning," he said angrily. "I don't ever want to see you where you don't belong again. Do you understand?"

"Yes." I nodded eagerly.

His eyes fell over my face once again, a slight furrow in his brow. "Officers," he called. "Escort the new recruit back to her division."

"Yes, Sergeant Wesley," the soldiers said, hurrying toward me.

I turned back as the guards escorted me away. "Thank you," I whispered quietly. His face was cast in shadow and just a flicker of his green eyes was visible. He stood alone in the hallway, watching me.

13

"UP, UP!" SCREAMED TUB. EVERYONE GROANED. IT WAS STILL pitch dark outside—at least an hour earlier than we usually woke. "Last one downstairs has to give me their rations!" she added. Suddenly the dorm was a flurry of activity as everyone jumped out of bed, hurrying to dress and race down to the dining hall. I took the stairs two at a time, my bootlaces untied.

Once I had my gruel, I ate quickly, holding my bowl close, guarding it with my body as we all did. Even when I was finished, my stomach still ached with hunger cramps. I had been in the army for a few weeks now. Training lasted from dawn to dusk every single day. Then it was work duties, which for me meant after-dinner cleanup with the girls from my bunk. The constant motion barely left me any time to think about, much less search for, Hollister. I was beginning to wonder if he was even here. At the end of each day, I was so tired I fell quickly into a leaden sleep, my muscles aching from the exercise. My last thoughts were always of my siblings. I wondered where their bodies had been buried, or if they had been sent to the Death Camps, where it was said you were ordered to dig your own grave.

I gulped down my last few sips of watered-down tea as Tub reappeared, leading us outside. At the outskirts of the woods we met up with the boys. The trees were still there, but they were skeletons now, charred and sodden, only bare branches and bark.

We stood there in the predawn darkness as Portia, Tub, and June passed us each a titanium sevil—ammunition was far too valuable to let us use guns—along with an empty tin cup in case we found any drinkable water.

"For those of you new to hunting," Portia announced, clearly relishing her role as leader, "let me remind you: This army is big, and it needs food. Hunting that food is *your* job." She stopped to look over the assembled soldiers, her eyes lingering for an extra moment on me.

"If you come back empty-handed, you'll be given double chores. The new soldier with the most kills will be promoted a full rank." She paused to let this sink in. "If you loot any of your fellow army members' weapons or kills, you will be punished. That is the most important rule—that you hunt your kill yourself. No sharing, no swapping, no bribing allowed. Is that understood?" Everyone nodded. I saw Sergeant Wesley moving through the boys' division with a pitcher of fresh water. He poured it into their cups, reminding them to drink it all. I immediately put my head down.

"Finally," Portia continued, "let me give you a few tips that will increase your chances of survival. There aren't any animals to be afraid of except for swamp snakes, so as long as you avoid swampy areas you'll most likely be fine. The bears have almost all starved to death. Your only real worry is the Roamers."

A gasp sounded through the crowd. "Relax," Tub cut in, giggling at everyone's obvious terror. "No one's been eaten . . . *yet.*"

"We meet back here at sundown," Portia went on undeterred. "Good luck."

One by one, she proceeded to call out the names of new

recruits, who placed their hands into a cloth sack and pulled out numbered slips of paper. The number indicated how many paces you had to step away from the group before you could begin hunting. Mine was 574.

I put the number in my pocket and looked out into the forest, wondering how far 574 steps would take me. Vashti squeezed my hand and whispered, "Good luck." Tub snickered as she began to count the numbers very slowly and loudly. I looked down at the muddy ground, then ahead at the trees. They all looked the same for miles and miles; bare, rotting trunks, with bark too damp to burn. I risked one glance back over my shoulder and saw Sergeant Wesley watching me. I whipped my head back around, my cheeks flaming, my face blank, as I walked off into the dead forest.

I counted the steps aloud as I walked, Tub's voice growing fainter and fainter until there was only the sound of my footsteps and breath. The trees looked menacing, their twisted branches reaching out to snatch at me. I looked at the sevil, amazed at how perfectly thin and razor-sharp it was. Cornelius Hollister had invented it, a deadly kind of sword that could slice through bone. I paused, turning it on its side to look at myself. Everything I saw reflected in the blade was devoid of color. Gray sky, gray trees—even my eyes looked gray.

My boots made a squelching sound as I stepped over mud and mulch, jumping across the wide roots of trees that the rain had laid bare. Mushrooms sprouted everywhere, small and white with red tops. I brushed my hand over them, searching for something edible, but these, like everything else in the forest, would lead only to death. I considered bringing some back and using them to poison Hollister, but decided against it. I didn't even know where he was, and when I did find him, I wanted to kill him with my own hands.

I stopped to examine the moss growing over the bark of a tree, emerald green and soft. I pulled off a section and chewed it slowly. It tasted of earth and grass, but it was clean and I knew it wouldn't kill me. As I moved on, I tripped over something in the mulch, and looked down to see a bit of cloth wedged beneath a rock. It was brown from the mud, but I could see the pattern of the cloth underneath—checked gingham, like the kind we had used for picnics. My breath caught and my eyes blurred. I blinked away my tears, holding tight to that wall of steel inside me, fighting the spark of the real me that threatened to break through. There was nothing left of that life, I thought angrily. There would be no more picnics with checked blankets.

Still, I ripped off a piece of the cloth and put it in my hunting sack.

I moved on, passing through a patch of burnt oaks, when I heard a rustling behind me. I froze, reaching carefully for the sevil, ready to strike, as a shadowy figure came closer. I spun around and stopped short.

Sergeant Wesley had his gun out, aimed at me. "Lower your weapon," he said slowly.

"I'll lower mine if you put your gun away," I challenged, eyeing him over the blade. If it came down to it, I could probably slice his jugular before he got a shot off.

"I don't take orders," he said, but he put his gun into its holster. "Your turn."

My hand started to shake as I kept the sevil held out in a defensive position. Why was he following me? Had he figured out who I was and come here to kill me? Had he seen me in the closet that night?

"What are you doing here?" I asked.

"I came to help," he replied evenly. His expression was so hard to read, I had no idea whether to believe him. "It's hard finding anything out here—unless you know where to look."

I hesitated, lowering the sevil. "You came to help me? Why?"

He didn't answer my question. "Come on. We need to keep moving. We've made noise in this area and scared away all the prey."

As he spoke, a cold wind shook the trees and the sky turned dark. Sergeant Wesley stopped, staring up at the blackening clouds with a frown. "I smell smoke," he said slowly. Smoke was the first sign of a Roamer camp.

I sniffed. "That's not wood smoke," I said. But it didn't have the sickly sweet tang of Roamer smoke either.

Suddenly the wind stopped. The air felt hot and still, like we were trapped in a room with no circulation. "Oh my God," he said, the realization hitting us both at once. "Run!"

We took off sprinting as a flash of lightning stretched from the sky to the ground, reaching out toward us like the bright white hand of a skeleton. And then everything seemed to explode.

I lay against the base of a tree, my head reeling from the sonic blast.

Then Sergeant Wesley was there, picking me up and hoisting me over his shoulders. "Don't pass out!" he yelled. I fought to stay conscious as the sky flashed red, then orange. A flame that looked like a house made of fire fell through the sky, and a baseball-size ember spun down to graze his left arm. It seared the fire-retardant fabric, turning it into a sizzling black mass of lava that melted on his skin. He dropped me and dove to the ground, rolling around to smother the jacket.

I took a deep breath, knowing I would have to run, and reached out a hand to pull him to his feet.

"There's a rock cave up this way!" he shouted over the roar of fire in the sky.

"We should be going downhill," I yelled.

"I know these woods," he insisted. "Follow me." Going uphill in lightning went against all my better judgment, but I swallowed my protests and followed.

We ducked into the cave just as a second sunball appeared, spiraling toward us. The whole hillside shook with the impact. I crouched at the mouth of the cave, catching my breath, unable to look away now that I was safe.

The sky was illuminated by a million flecks of light, sparkling and falling to the ground in a shower as thick as rain. I hadn't seen this much light since before the Seventeen Days. "It's beautiful," I said softly, in awe. Like sparklers. Like fireworks.

"Beautiful, but dangerous," Wesley agreed, his gaze lingering on me for longer than necessary. The sparks continued to fall from the sky around us, growing smaller and further apart until some were only the size of the flame on a matchstick.

Neither of us spoke. I tried to keep from looking at his gun. He kept it secured in its holster, but my sevil was melted and twisted, totally useless. If he wanted to kill me, I would have no way of stopping him.

There was a moment of quiet in the sky. Then as quickly as it had come, the fire vanished and the rains began. Pounding gray rains, turning the charred forests to wet ash. The rain fell in drops the size of icicles, spearing the earth.

"If it wasn't for all the rain, England would be on fire," Sergeant Wesley said as he pulled off his jacket, wincing as the fabric peeled away from the bright red burn where the fireball had touched his arm.

I gasped. "That looks painful."

"It is."

Remembering the gingham cloth I had found, I took it from my sack and held it outside in the cold rain.

"Here." I leaned forward. Sergeant Wesley held out his arm, but I noticed he pressed his other hand tight to his gun as I approached. I wrapped the cool cloth around the burn. He gritted his teeth but didn't speak. As I turned his arm over to tie the knot, I noticed something on his forearm—the crossed sword and sevil of the New Guard.

I tightened the knot quickly, my eyes lowered. "Thanks," he said.

"It's nothing," I answered quickly. "You helped me too."

We fell silent again, watching the rain. When it had slowed to a fine mist, we made our way out of the cave.

He walked ahead quietly through the fallen trees. The air smelled like rain mixed with burnt wood. "Careful," Sergeant Wesley warned as we edged along a cliff.

"I'm fine," I protested, though looking down made me a little dizzy.

"Here," he said, reaching for me. Reluctantly, I held out my hand toward his. His fingers wrapped around mine, and he guided me carefully away from the cliff, holding tight as we descended the slope.

When we were safely away from the cliff, he loosened his grip, and I let my hand drop to my side. A crow flew overhead out of the lonely gray sky. It was the first living thing I'd seen all day. We watched as the bird circled lazily above the high branches of a tree. Sergeant Wesley pulled out his pistol, aiming straight at it. But instead of shooting, he lowered his arm to his side.

"Why didn't you kill it?" I asked.

"It's circling its nest," he muttered, "bringing its hatchlings food." I looked at him in surprise. "I mean, we need those birds to grow up so they can be food someday too. We'll find something else."

We walked on, continuing down the slope of the hill in the gray midday light. It was strange how quickly the sunball had come and gone. I wondered if any of the other soldiers had been caught in it, and what would've happened to me had I been alone.

Suddenly he grabbed my arm, holding his finger up to his lips. I listened, and then I heard it too—the sound of light footsteps, coming from behind the trees. He pulled me behind him, holding out the pistol, ready to shoot.

A fox appeared from behind a pile of brush, followed by its offspring. They were so beautiful, so still, looking at us with a mixture of curiosity and fear. Once when I was walking on my own through the woods in Scotland, one had followed me, nibbling at the bushes. They were so rare that I'd considered it a small sign of good luck.

Sergeant Wesley turned to me. "I haven't seen a fox since I was six or seven years old."

I shook my head. "I thought they were all dead."

"Maybe they've just been hiding."

"The sunball probably made them flee their dens," I agreed.

He dropped his pistol on the ground as he knelt down, holding out the palm of his hand, murmuring at the foxes not to be afraid.

I knelt down next to him. In my sack I still had the small lunch I'd been issued that morning. I broke off part of the potato, laying it on the ground for them like a peace offering.

The mother fox walked up slowly, her kit following close by her side. They stopped a few feet away, eyeing us cautiously.

"It's all right," I said softly, tossing the potato toward them. They must have been starving because they ate it right away. When they were finished, they stepped closer, moving slowly, silently.

I reached out tentatively and touched the baby fox's head. It leaned in and nuzzled my palm. I laughed, feeling the coarse reddish fur between its ears as it turned its face to the side, like a cat, enjoying being scratched.

I looked at Sergeant Wesley in disbelief that they had come so near, so trustingly. For the first time since my father's death, I felt something like hope.

Just then a glimmer shot through the air. The mother fox went still, its eyes wide open and staring at me. Before I even had time to react, a second arrow sent the baby to the ground, dead alongside the body of its mother.

"Bull's-eye!"

Standing behind an old, rotting tree, lowering her weapon, was Portia.

14

PORTIA WALKED TOWARD US, HER BOW AT HER SIDE, GRINNING.
"Sorry to disturb your little nature walk, but I've always
wanted a fox stole."

I stared at the bodies of the foxes. Their still-open eyes
were glassy, the silver-colored arrows piercing their small
bodies. Only a moment ago they were alive, part of the
world.

"Why would you do that?" Sergeant Wesley said
angrily.

"Survival of the fittest." Portia pulled the arrows from
the bodies of the foxes. She wiped the red blood on her
riding pants, letting out a sigh. "The baby's probably

too small for a stole, but I couldn't just leave it without its mother, could I? What child wants to live without its mother?"

Sergeant Wesley stared at her, his eyes narrowed in anger. "That wasn't necessary, Portia."

"Nothing is *necessary*," she laughed. "And anyway, what are you doing with my new recruit?" She turned toward me and raised her bow in a single, fluid motion so the next thing I knew, she was aiming directly at the center of my forehead. I held my breath, feeling suddenly frozen in place. "As for you, fresh, I thought I told you to stay out of trouble." I stared at her hard eyes as she paused for dramatic effect. "Maybe I'll just save us both the effort and shoot you now. A routine hunting accident."

"That's enough," Sergeant Wesley snapped. "You know better."

She sighed, blowing her bangs up in the air as she lowered her bow. "Lighten up, Wes. You used to have a sense of humor."

"Why'd you even come here? Are you following me?" A tightness pulled at his lips.

She paused, then broke into a smile, baring all of her perfect, white teeth. "Don't flatter yourself. I wasn't following you, I was following the foxes."

"Well then," he said angrily, "if you wouldn't mind taking your carcasses with you . . ."

Portia picked up the dead foxes by their tails, dropping them into her hunting sack and slinging it over her shoulder. "See you back at the bunk, *Polly*," she added, giving me one last look.

Sergeant Wesley stared hard into the woods, watching her until she was gone.

The wind picked up, swirling with the ashes like dark ghosts, then vanishing. The sky was gray and still, like gun-metal.

Eventually, he spoke. "I'm sorry about Portia," he offered. "She wasn't always like that. She used to be . . ." He paused, searching for the right word. "Different."

"You seem to have known her a long time," I said carefully.

"Yes, I have. And I haven't given up hope that the old Portia will come back."

I knew how he felt. Wishing, waiting. "I understand."

He looked at me, as if waiting for me to go on. "It was my brother. He was . . . sick," I continued vaguely. "I used to hold on to the hope that he would get better. Even though there was no cure for him, I still hoped." I remembered how

I used to be so certain that Jamie would one day run and play like a normal boy.

Sergeant Wesley looked up sharply, a troubled expression on his face. He opened his mouth as though to speak, then closed it.

"What?" I asked.

He shook his head. "Nothing. It's getting late. We should head back."

He led me quickly through the woods, following a trail I never would have found. It was almost completely dark out when we saw the flames from the bonfire rising up between the trees and smelled the smoke filling the air.

"Here." He handed me a pigeon he'd shot on the way back. "Remember the rules."

"Thank you, Sergeant."

"Please," he said. "Call me Wesley. And you're welcome. Now you'd better go by yourself from here."

He turned away, and I stumbled forward to camp, where Tub was checking the kills everyone had brought back. I held out the pigeon Wesley had given me. When they saw me, the other girls fell silent. Tub looked at Portia, then back at me.

"You killed a pigeon?" Portia asked, her eyes narrowing.

I nodded.

"Or did Wesley do it for you?" she said with a pointed sneer.

"Here, take it," I said in defeat, tossing the dead bird at her. She caught it with a look of surprise. "You can have it. I'm not hungry."

Later that night I stood in the girls' bunk, staring down at my bed. The bodies of the two foxes were laid across it, the blood from their wounds staining the dark green blanket.

"A little prezzy," a voice sliced behind me through the silence. I whipped around as Portia and Tub appeared.

"Do you sew?" Portia asked with a smirk. "I'm looking for someone to make me my fox stole."

"And a jacket for me," Tub added.

I held my hand over my mouth, feeling sick. The dead mother fox and her baby lay on my bed, their bodies smelling sour, tiny black flies crawling in their ears and eyes.

I threw out the carcasses, but the scent of death lingered, rising up around me in the night.

15

I STANED OUT HI THE FIELDS AS THE TRUCKS CARRIED US DOWN
the dirt road leading away from the palace. We had been told we
were going on a raid in a village called Mulberry. I hadn't asked
questions. I knew better by now. It had been three days since
Portia had left the dead foxes on my bed, and I had mostly tried to
stay out of her way since then. The mantra I had made for myself
my first night had become more important than ever. *Stay calm.
Don't ask questions. Be patient.* But I felt her eyes always upon me.

The moon was bright, and I saw windowless buildings
surrounded by a high barbed-wire fence. I turned to the
soldier next to me. He had bright brown eyes and only looked
about fifteen.

"Do you know what those buildings are for?" I asked him quietly.

The boy peered out. "I don't know." He shrugged. "Never seen them before."

By the side of each building, a giant trench had been dug into the earth and filled with loose soil. I pressed my face close to the glass. Sticking out from the soil, I thought I saw a human hand.

I put my forehead on my knees, feeling sick with dread. This must be where the bodies of the dead prisoners were taken and buried. Were my siblings' bodies dumped in the dirt pile? Could that have been Mary's hand, or Jamie's?

The trucks rumbled over the broken-down highways for miles, then down narrow country lanes overgrown on either side with hedgerows. Suddenly the trucks lurched to a stop, throwing us forward in our seats.

Outside stood a small whitewashed cottage with a thatched roof like a brown cap. The windows of the cottage flickered with candlelight. A pea-stone path led through the front garden trellis to an arched doorway. There was a small boxwood garden and a stone birdbath. When I saw the red letterbox on the door, I knew exactly where we were.

Sergeant Fax ordered us out of the trucks, then stormed up the path through the garden. He kicked open the cottage door, sending it slamming against the wall, and ordered his troops to march inside.

I forced my feet forward, left, right, over the threshold of the home of the two women who had raised me. The first thing that hit me was the scent of tea and toast and tapioca pudding. It reminded me of my childhood. We entered a cozy sitting room where two old women sat in front of a small fire. A gray cat looked up from where she sat nestled on the arm of one of the women's chairs.

Even though I hadn't seen them in years, I recognized Nora and Rita immediately. Not that they would recognize me now, wearing the uniform of the New Guard, with my haunted, hungry face. My heart thudded dully in my chest. They had once bathed me and fed me and read me bedtime stories. Now here I was, pointing a weapon at them.

Their faces were full of confusion as they looked up, books still open on their laps.

"We have come for the royal crown," Sergeant Fax bellowed, his thick neck bulging. "We know it has been hidden here."

My knife slipped a fraction of an inch as my mind raced. Could the royal crown really be here? And if so, who would have given the New Guard this information? The only person who might know was Mary, and she would never endanger

Nora and Rita. Unless she had no other choice. I turned away, the thought of Mary and Jamie alive but being brutally tortured too much to bear.

Surprisingly, Rita smiled at Sergeant Fax, then at the soldiers circling the sitting room. She wore a matching lavender sweater set and trousers. A carved wooden cane leaned against the arm of the sofa. Framed pictures of friends and family hung on the walls. I recognized the one of Mary and me at the pond in Hyde Park, having a picnic.

I stepped back behind the line of soldiers so they would have less chance of seeing me. I cast my eyes downward and stared at the oval woven rug.

"I am very sorry, sir, but I cannot give you the Windsor crown," Rita said calmly. "I do not have it, and even if I did, it is not mine to give away."

"I don't know if you heard me correctly," the sergeant repeated, his words falling like bricks. "I said, hand it over."

Rita smiled serenely and stood, holding her thin hands clasped in front of her. Nora glanced up at her, a worried look in her eyes.

"Quite possibly it was you who did not understand my reply. I said, I am very sorry, but I am afraid I cannot give you the crown. But I can offer you a nice cup of tea, and I just baked a batch of cheddar scones."

A muffled snicker went through the room. I could even see Wesley, who stood by the door, trying not to smile.

A shot rang out, followed by a scream. Sergeant Fax had shot the cat perched on the arm of Nora's chair. Blood was splattered all over Nora's hands and face. My stomach clenched.

"Enough chattering! Give me the jewels now! Or you'll end up like the cat."

Nora began to shake uncontrollably. Without thinking, I pushed my way forward to help her, but Wesley grabbed my wrist to stop me.

"Don't move," he ordered, in his sergeant's voice, and I took a deep breath through my mouth, calming myself.

Rita stared back at Sergeant Fax, the fireplace burning quietly behind her.

Nora looked up at her. All the color had drained from her face and tears were running down her cheeks. "Please, Rita, give them the crown," she said softly. She seemed unable to move. She sat there in her chair, letting the cat bleed to death beside her.

Without speaking, Rita did as Nora asked. She walked as though in a trance to the bedroom, where we heard the sound of a safe being opened. A moment later, she returned carrying a carved wooden box with a silver keyhole. I almost laughed out loud. The symbol of my father's rule had been hidden in a small wooded cottage with only two old ladies for protection. I wondered if my father had moved the jewels when he realized just how powerful Cornelius Hollister was becoming, imagining that no one would think to look for them here.

Sergeant Fax tore the box from her hand, taking the key and unlocking it. He scanned the inside compartments, pulling out the main treasure, the Windsor coronation crown, which Hollister would need to proclaim himself king.

But first he would have to end the Windsor line of succession.

Fax raised his gun, aiming it at Nora's head. Nora closed her eyes. "Good-bye, Rita," she whispered. The skin on her eyelids was as thin and wrinkled as tissue paper.

I pictured myself taking the knife from my belt and slitting Sergeant Fax's thick neck. As he lay dying, I would tell him that his leader, Cornelius Hollister, would never wear the crown, that it would never belong to him.

"Stop!" a voice said firmly, and Sergeant Fax turned his head. Wesley pushed his way roughly through the crowd of soldiers. Sergeant Fax lowered his gun, looking at him.

"Let's not waste the bullets on them, Fax. We got what we came for."

After a long, tense pause, Sergeant Fax nodded, and the soldiers turned to file out of the house, following Wesley's lead.

The troops marched through the cottage door, stomping along the winding pea-stone path. I marched in line, following them, when someone grabbed my shoulder.

Sergeant Fax gestured to an oil painting of lush green woods and a waterfall. "Take that painting from the wall."

"Me?" I asked dumbly.

"Yes, you!" His crimson face was so close, I could feel his spit land on my cheek and winced in disgust.

"Yes, sir," I said, saluting him.

I turned toward the painting. From the corner of my eye I could see Nora, still sitting in her chair. It was as though she had been petrified, turned into a marble statue.

I felt her eyes on me as I made my way across the room to the wall behind the sofa. The greens and blues came into focus and I realized it was the waterfall and the old wide trees where we would practice our dives back in Scotland. The picture seemed to come alive as I stared into it; I could feel the breeze, smell the grass, hear the rush of the water falling and our voices as we swam and dove from the cliff. "Hurry up!" Sergeant Fax shouted at me, and I grabbed the frame, taking it down from the hook as his troops ransacked other parts of the cottage, grabbing the table and chairs, dishes, anything they could carry.

I turned from the wall, facing Nora. She stared at me curiously, as though she recognized something, a part of me, but could not place it.

"I'm sorry," I murmured, glancing back to make sure Sergeant Fax wasn't listening, then fled.

Inside the truck, the soldiers broke open bottles of liquor they had stolen. They sang the anthem of the New Guard, retelling moments of the siege and of other raids while passing around the bottles and cheering as if stealing from unarmed old ladies was some heroic feat. Refusing the scotch when it came to me, I took one last look back. The small house with the thin wisp of smoke from the chimney looked like a page from a children's picture book.

I dug my fingernails into my palm, just to remind myself I could still feel. I had harmed the kindest women in the world, women who were like second mothers to my siblings and me after our own mother had died.

The truck rattled along the dirt and stone roads. The moon was dim in the sky, the stars faded. The miles and miles of fields stretched out like the sea. I felt hollow and empty, unable even to cry.

A noise above me yanked me out of my daze, and I looked

up to see Wesley slide into the seat beside mine. "Polly," he said, an edge to his voice.

"What do you want?" I asked angrily, turning away to hide the tears that threatened to spill from my eyes.

"I shouldn't have had to stop you tonight. Don't you know how dangerous it is to disobey an officer?"

I heard my breath as I inhaled and felt the night air cool and damp in my lungs. Why would I cry now? After everything that happened tonight, why now? I felt myself almost give in, but I clenched my fists and held my breath, reminding myself how much I hated everyone in the New Guard.

"I can't believe what they did to . . ." I caught myself before saying their names. "What makes Sergeant Fax think he can treat people like that, killing their cat, taking their possessions?" I was shaking with disgust.

Wesley glanced around the truck to make sure no one was listening to our conversation. He put his arms on my shoulders, steadying me. "Polly, one step out of line and it'll be your head, don't you see? I'm trying to help you," he whispered as the trucks came to a halting stop.

We disembarked in front of the palace gates, where Portia, Tub, and some of the higher-ranking officers were waiting to unload the more valuable items we had taken from the cottage. Wesley nodded at them as he stepped away, heading toward his squadron to lead them to their bunks for the night. But Portia stood there, her eyes like darts as she stared straight at me. The way an owl might perch on a branch, still as a statue, eyeing its prey.

16

WHEN I WALKED INTO THE DORM I KNEW RIGHT AWAY SOMETHING was wrong. All the girls except for Vashti were gathered in a circle in the center of the room, but there were no cards in sight. The air felt thick with a strange sense of anticipation.

"I'm really beginning to wonder about you," Portia announced, speaking slowly, as if every word were a candy she wanted to savor. "You haven't started my fox stole yet—and I don't even think you know how to sew. You can't clean. Your accent switches back and forth from Scottish to posh Londoner." She said the last in a high-pitched, nasal imitation of my voice, and everyone laughed. Then her voice dropped an octave lower. "Honestly, I don't know what

131

Sergeant Wesley sees in you. He's slummed around with recruits before, but not like this."

I stood still, without even shifting my weight or glancing away for one second. My heart hammered in my chest.

Tub came to Portia's side. "Are you a spy from the Resistance?"

Portia rolled her eyes, then walked forward to take my chin in her hand, turning my face so I was forced to look her in the eye. "I doubt she's smart enough to be a spy. This is just a stupid girl who can't even follow simple orders." Everyone laughed again. She leaned in close, grabbing my chin tighter, leaning to whisper in my ear so only I could hear her. "Tell me why you're here."

"I'm here to fight for the New Guard," I said loudly.

"Are you really? Then why did you hesitate when you were face-to-face with a Resistance fighter on Death Night? Are you pro-Resistance or just a coward?"

"I'm here to fight for the New Guard," I repeated, my face stony, impassive.

Portia dropped her hand from my chin. "Prove it, then."

I stepped back. "What?"

"Prove it!"

Portia pushed up her right sleeve. On the pale under-side of her arm was a tattoo of the crossed sevil and sword.

Before I knew what was happening, Tub and June had me in their arms. June dug her knees in my back. Portia stood next to her, holding my wrists in her hand, tying them tightly with rope.

They pushed me into the toilets. The tiled floor blurred beneath my feet as Portia took out a long pair of scissors from a shelf.

She grabbed the back of my neck. I didn't make a sound—I wasn't going to give them the satisfaction. I felt the cool blade of the scissors next to my scalp and heard the clipping sound, then saw the strands of my hair falling like rain around my knees on the bathroom floor.

Portia pushed me in front of the mirror. "What do you think?"

They had sheared it close to my head, so close the skin on my scalp showed through.

Tub and June were bent over laughing, holding their stomachs, their faces bright red.

"Sergeant Wesley certainly won't be flirting with *you* anymore," June snickered.

When I looked in the mirror what struck me most wasn't the short hair, haphazardly hacked off close to my scalp, but the desolate look in my eyes. I was a shadow of my former self.

"I love it," I said, turning to Portia and the others. "I've been meaning to get a haircut."

But my sarcasm only enraged her. Her beautiful face became contorted and red.

"I'm not finished yet," she spat. "June, hold her down."

June pushed me to the floor, the back of my head slamming against the marble. She pinned my shoulders down and Tub sat on my legs, her tremendous weight impossible to move. I kicked and squirmed wildly but then June pulled out her sevil, placing it above my chest so that if I moved even an inch the blade would cut through my skin. I squeezed my hands in fists at my side.

From the corner of my eye I watched Portia standing by the cauldron of water that sat over the coals. She held a wire hanger in her hand, untwisting the metal to make it straight. She placed the wire beneath the coals.

"Please let go of me," I begged, hating the desperate sound of my voice but unable to stop. "Please get off of me."

"Keep her down!" Portia screamed. She gazed into the red coals with a frightening intensity. The flames were reflected in the dark pupils of her eyes. She smiled at the flames, relishing the moment.

Not my eyes, I prayed. *Don't let her blind me.*

She pulled the blazing red wire from the coals, holding it in front of my face.

"Keep still," she ordered. "If I mess up I'll have to do it again."

Portia lowered herself to her knees beside me, holding the glowing red wire in her hand.

First I felt the heat, like putting a finger over a flame. Then I felt the searing as she pressed the burning wire against my cheek. I bolted up in pain, writhing to free myself only to have Tub slam my head back against the floor. The burning pain pierced my whole body like nothing I'd ever felt before. Somebody cried out; it must have been me. The room went red and then black. The last sound I heard was the girls' echoing laughter.

17

IT WAS THE PAIN THAT WOKE ME.

Cringing at the feeling of hot needles stabbing into the skin below my right eye, I turned my face to press my cheek against the cold marble floor. But it was hardly a relief. I took deep, shuddering breaths to brace myself, my eyes still shut tight. Unsteadily, I pushed myself up to stand and held myself over the sink.

On my face below my right eye the skin rose up in blisters, forming a crude image of a crossed sevil and sword.

They had branded me with the symbol of the New Guard.

I touched the raw, burnt skin and bit back a cry of pain.

Even alone in the bathroom I couldn't let Portia win. I would not show her the weakness she wanted to see in me.

I steadied myself on the sink. I needed to leave, tonight. If I stayed here any longer, trying to accomplish this hopeless mission, I would be killed. I reached for the door, but it wouldn't give. I was locked in.

Taking deep breaths to fight my rising panic, I looked around for an escape. I wasn't sure how long I'd been unconscious, but I knew Portia would come back eventually. There was a small round window on the south-facing wall that looked out over the treetops into the still night. The window was thick glass inlaid with wire mesh. We were on the third floor. If I jumped, I would be lucky to survive the fall.

I lifted the cauldron awkwardly from the coals and smashed it against the glass, wincing and holding my breath at the heavy crash that resounded through the bathroom. When no one came running, I hit at the glass, again and again until the thick pane shattered in pieces to the floor, leaving just the mesh in place.

I began tearing out the mesh until there was a gap large enough for me to crawl through. On the window ledge I paused, gripping the stone casing with my bare, bleeding hands and staring down at the drop to the ground. The air was still, the black night spreading out through the sky like a pool of spilled ink, not a star in sight. The only light came from a row of torches bobbing underneath the window— soldiers on patrol. I leaned back, hiding in the shadows, dizzy and sick from the pain and fear.

The sound of dripping water came from my left. I looked over to see the gleam of a copper drainpipe beneath a heavy growth of vines. The pipes had recently been installed to collect rainwater from the roof for drinking. I doubted it would be strong enough to hold me, but it was better than nothing. I leaned out until I almost fell over. The vines were just out of reach.

I took a deep breath, trying to calculate the distance. Then all at once I released my grip on the window casing and sprang off the windowsill.

I slid down rapidly, ignoring the pain in my fingers, still studded with glass and bits of mesh, as I grabbed at the vines. My feet braced against the wall, scrambling to find footing. Finally I found purchase in the rough stones and thick vines. I clung to the vines, willing myself not to scream out in pain.

And so, inch by inch, I slid down the drainpipe like a fire pole, until I finally felt solid ground beneath me.

I pressed my back to the palace wall, glancing in both

directions. The barbed-wire fence rose up out of the shadows ten feet in front of me. There was no way to climb over the rotating spikes on top without being mangled, and I couldn't possibly dig my way under. It would have to be the woods. I retied the laces of my boots and took off in a sprint, away from the palace, toward the wall of solid darkness that was the barren trees.

I was almost across the field when a figure materialized before me, knocking me to the ground.

"Hands behind your back!" a harsh male voice cried out. My throbbing burn pressed painfully into the dirt as the soldier put his foot on my neck, holding me down. Another soldier approached with a burning torch and tied my hands behind my back. I winced at the feel of the rope on my wounded palms, but I tried to stay utterly still.

The first soldier, a sergeant, turned me roughly around to look at my face. "What's your name?" he commanded.

"An escapee," the young guard said as he twisted my wrists at a sharp, painful angle. I said nothing.

"Get up," the sergeant snapped, pulling me to my feet and shoving me forward.

They prodded me with their sevils, herding me forward across the palace grounds into the stark fields that led to the Death Camps. The sounds that had haunted me, the agonizing cries of pain and rattle of chains, grew louder as we marched. As we approached the gate, I saw a long line of people shuffling out into the field, bound at the ankles. A soldier handed each of them a shovel.

Why don't they use the shovels as weapons? I thought. But these prisoners were skin and bone, dragging their shovels behind them despondently. There was no fight left in them.

"Start digging!" a soldier shouted, walking behind them and hitting the slower ones on the head with the flat of his sevil. The sound of the metal against their skulls echoed in the night. I watched in horror as the soldier lined up the prisoners and proceeded to fire at their heads, one after the other. They fell into the shallow holes like human dominoes.

I put my hand across my mouth as the truth hit me. These men had been forced to dig their own graves. Once I walked through that gate, I would never get out.

Another soldier stood guard at the gate of the Death Camps. I blinked in the sudden light of the coal lantern, certain that my eyes were deceiving me. It was Wesley. He met my gaze, then looked quickly away.

"Barth and Harbor," he addressed them. "Aren't you on front gate duty?"

"We have an escapee," Sergeant Barth said.

"Hand her over," Wesley ordered, without so much as looking at me. "And get back to your posts now."

"Sir!" The two soldiers saluted him and turned to jog back toward the fields.

When they were gone, he loosened his grip on my shoulders and turned me to face him. I stared down at the ground, but I felt his eyes burning into me like the wire of the clothes hanger. I had never felt so ashamed—of my face, of my decisions, of how stupid I had been to think I could come here and kill Cornelius Hollister. Instead, I had been branded with his symbol.

"Who did this to you?" he asked quietly. "Was it Portia?"

I said nothing. Tears pooled in my eyes, blurring my vision.

"Move quickly and don't say anything," Wesley ordered as he pushed me forward. The steel wire fence of the Death Camps rose up sharply in the light of the moon. I stopped, whirling around to face him.

"How can you live with yourself, working for this army?" I asked in a trembling voice, staring deep into his eyes. "If you're going to kill me, go ahead and do it now."

He pushed me forward. "Didn't you hear me?" he hissed. "I said, don't speak. Keep walking." The moonlight fell across his angular cheekbones and lit up the dark hollows of his eyes.

We had passed the camps and were now walking down the dark field toward a windowless brick building. "Where are you taking me?" I said through clenched teeth.

He pulled me to a stop and began to untie the rope binding my wrists.

"You're not taking me to the camps?" My voice was filled with confusion.

He took a second gun from his uniform and placed it in my palm. "Do you know how to shoot?"

"Yes."

"There's a full round in there. Don't let go of it. If we get separated, if the Roamers get you, just shoot them. Don't hesitate or they'll kill you first."

I nodded mechanically and wrapped my fingers around the grip, wincing at the pain as I placed my finger experimentally on the trigger.

"I'm taking you somewhere safe, but we have to go through the woods to get there," Wesley went on. "And we need to be quiet and careful. If I'm caught helping you, we'll both be killed."

I raised my eyes to his. I wanted to trust him, but what if

this was just an elaborate trap? "Why are you helping me?" I asked.

He looked toward the Death Camps in the distance. "You're not the only person here with something to hide, Eliza."

18

THE SOUND OF MY REAL NAME MADE ME FREEZE. AN OWL HOOTED overhead, perched like a statue on the limb of a tree. Everything was in slow motion, as though time had come unhinged.

"You know who I am," I said, but my voice was scarcely audible. The night air chilled my skin. It was so dark I almost couldn't see Wesley in front of me.

"Yes."

"Does anyone else know?"

"Not that I know of."

I stumbled back a step. "How? When . . . ?" I shook my head before asking the question that had plagued me for weeks. "Why did you let me escape that night in the palace?"

He nodded, as if he had expected this. "I looked in your eyes, and . . . I just couldn't do it." He paused, fumbling for words. "Please trust me."

I thought about the times he'd been alone with me, with a weapon, when I'd been unarmed. If he'd wanted to kill me, he would have done it by now. Finally I nodded. "Where are we going?" I asked, still dazed, as we walked together back toward the center of camp.

"You'll see," he said somberly.

Inside the windowless cinder-block building, Cornelius Hollister's warhorses thrashed behind the thick bars of their stalls. They stood at least a full head taller than regular horses, and their eyes were bloodred and filled with rage. Their steel-shod hooves pawed the ground angrily. They butted their heads against the railings of their stalls, so hard some of them had worn the skin bare, the bone coming through.

Wesley saddled a black-and-white mare while I hid inside the shadow of the doorway, keeping guard. The saddle and reins hung from posts in the wall, so thick and plated they looked more like armor than riding gear. I thought of Jasper and shivered. These creatures had been bred for war, beaten since they were born. They were machines of anger and destruction.

I watched Wesley put a spiked bit in the mare's mouth and stifled a cry of protest. "You can't use that!" I whispered loudly. "It'll hurt her!"

"I know." He nodded sadly. "But they don't respond to the regular bits." He pulled the huge horse out of the stall and into the courtyard, hoisting me up onto the saddle. "Her name's Caligula," he said. "She's one of the fastest."

He jumped up in front of me, and Caligula took off in a sudden gallop across the fields. I grabbed him tightly around the waist.

As we melted into the woods, Caligula slowed to a canter, gliding easily over root beds and fallen tree trunks. The sounds of the forest at night filled the silence that fell between us. A family of bats flew past like a small dark storm, screeching as they glided by.

After what seemed like an hour, Caligula finally fell back into a trot, picking her way carefully around the edge of a shiny silver lake. Wesley frowned in confusion. "Strange," he murmured. "I haven't seen this water before."

"It looks like a loch where we used to swim in Scotland," I said, thinking of the lake where Mary, Polly, and I had spent so many carefree summer days. We would pack a picnic and play games, and practice diving off a high tree branch that hung over the water. Jamie would sit, a blanket covering him because he shivered even in the summer, scoring our dives.

"Let's stop here," Wesley said. "We need water anyway." He dismounted and tied Caligula's reins to a branch. "And we should put some cold water on your burn," he added, making his way down the path.

A ripple in the water dipped, then vanished before I could even be sure I had seen it. Was it a fish? I hadn't seen a live fish in years. I could spear it and cook it over the fire—Polly's father, George, had taught me how to spear salmon when I was little. I followed Wesley down to the edge of the lake, watching for another ripple. As I moved closer I saw the water was a strange and beautiful silver, reflecting the light as if it glowed from within.

Wesley knelt down and cupped his hands to drink. I suddenly realized why the water had a silver sheen.

For a split second, I considered letting him drink. One sip was all it would take to poison him, and I still didn't know whether I could trust him or where he was leading me.

"Wait—stop!" I cried out at the last moment. "That's a mercury pool! It will kill you if you drink it. We shouldn't even be breathing this close to it."

Wesley stepped back quickly, his eyes wide as he looked at the silver poison. At the water's edge I saw what I had missed: the deformed and dead bodies of water creatures floating in the shallows. Fish with fins where eyes should have been, frogs with no legs, eels with heads at both ends.

I looked up through the woods across the lake. Hidden within the overgrowth of vines was a windowless cinder-block structure with the enormous CX logo. One of the thousands of Chemex plants, where everything from shampoo to lawn fertilizer to Death Clouds had been manufactured before the Seventeen Days. In the wake of the destruction, their deadly chemicals had leaked out to poison the earth for miles around.

"I was thinking that it was the most beautiful water I'd ever seen," Wesley said, his voice quavering. "I would have drunk it if you hadn't warned me." He looked up. "Thank you."

"Of course," I said, ashamed I had even considered letting him drink. "Thank you for . . ." I wanted to say *sparing my life*, but instead I said, "For keeping my secret."

I looked out at the lake. Wesley was right. It was the most beautiful water I had ever seen. Beautiful, yet deadly. Like so much of the world.

My face still hurt, but it was now my hands that were throbbing with a deep and painful intensity. Blood was seeping slowly from the places where small shards of glass and bits of steel mesh had dug into my skin. We had been riding for at least an hour since the mercury pool. I hoped we didn't have much longer to go.

"Almost there," Wesley said, answering my unspoken thought. He leaned to the left and pushed aside a thick clump of bushes, revealing a narrow path between the heavy walls of vines. Caligula walked through carefully, her breath making small puffs in the frosty air.

In a clearing ahead was a stone cottage with a thatched roof. Moss covered the outside walls, the paint peeled in sheets on the front door, and the iron casement windows were covered in spiderwebs and vines.

"Does anyone . . . live here?" I asked quietly. I'd heard that the Roamers had a dark, isolated house where they kept their captives alive, locked up and waiting to be eaten, like a human refrigerator.

"No one's here. It's safe," Wesley assured me. But I held tight to the gun, ignoring the pain in my hand, as he tethered Caligula to a post and drew her a bucket of water from the stone well.

"How did you know this was here? How can you be sure no one is hiding inside?"

"No one else knows about it." Wesley took a key from

his pocket and unlatched the front door. I hesitantly followed him inside.

The air in the cottage was cold and still and smelled of mildew and damp earth. I stood in a small sitting room, where a faded, rose-patterned loveseat and two wicker chairs faced a stone fireplace. Wesley reached down to light a wax candle sitting on the coffee table. A few brown moths circled the firelight, flying dangerously close to the flame.

"I'm going to make a fire," he announced. "It's cold in here." I held my hands in front of me, nervous about being in the woods at night. I looked at the windows and door. The glass panes could easily be broken, the door smashed with a few blows of an axe. I still clutched the gun, almost for comfort, the way a child might hold their mother's hand.

"You can put down the gun, you know." He gestured to my hand. "I'm not going to hurt you."

I hesitated a moment, then set it on the table. "I know." And I realized that I believed it. I was safe here with him. "I was worried the Roamers might come."

Wesley looked at me thoughtfully, as though considering whether I was telling the truth. "They won't come. I promise."

I sat down on the worn loveseat, glancing around for some clue as to where we were. Cheerful cherry beams crossed the low ceiling and a warm oval rug covered the floor.

The windows were hung with dusty, pale yellow half-curtains trimmed with lace. In the circle of candlelight, I saw small rosebuds on the tablecloth.

"Whose house was this?" I asked.

"My mother's," he replied as he fed twigs and branches into the fire. I waited for him to go on, but instead he looked at my hands. "You should wash out those cuts. I'll heat some water—go look in the kitchen cupboard and see if there's any salt."

When I came back into the sitting room holding a box of salt, Wesley had drawn another pail of water from the well and was heating it in a pot over the fire. The shadows cast by the red and yellow flames danced around the room. Even though it was clear that the cottage hadn't been used in years, it seemed lived in and well loved.

"Did you read the Peter Rabbit books when you were young?" I asked. "That's what this place reminds me of—the Rabbits' burrow."

"I'm glad." He began to smile. I realized it was the first time I had ever seen him smile.

"You look different when you smile," I said softly.

His eyes caught mine, resting on them for a moment before looking down at my bloody hands. "Come here." He gestured for me to sit on the carpet in front of the fireplace.

"This is going to sting, but it's the only way to clean out those cuts." He poured salt into the now-hot water and crouched down behind me, reaching around to circle my wrists and lower my hands slowly into the pot. I gasped at the shock. I closed my eyes and tried to shut out the pain. As the clear water reddened with blood and the bits of glass and metal loosened from my skin, I began to feel acutely aware of Wesley, still kneeling there behind me, his breath tickling my ear.

He stood up abruptly. "Stay here. I'm going to see if I can find us anything to eat."

After some searching, Wesley returned with several cans of vegetable soup. "Expired, but they should still be good," he said quietly. He moved aside the pot of water to place the soup over the flame. When it was hot, he ladled it into two wooden bowls. I wrapped my hands in the makeshift bandages he'd cut from a sheet, hopeful at how clean the wounds looked, and sipped the steaming broth directly from the bowl. Already I felt stronger.

Wesley was heating a fresh pot of salted water over the fire. When it was just about boiling, he dipped in another strip of the torn bedsheet. "Okay," he said. "Now the burn."

He reached out and cleaned my cheek with the warm

cloth, his touch gentle. "I can't believe Portia did this," he said quietly.

I paused and then spoke evenly. "You were together once, weren't you?"

Wesley started to laugh, a sad, bitter laugh, and shook his head. He looked me squarely in the eye. "Portia and I were never together," he said slowly. "Eliza, she's my sister."

My mouth opened in surprise. I thought suddenly of their matching dark green eyes, dark blond hair, high cheekbones. I couldn't believe I hadn't seen it before. "But you're so . . . different."

He reapplied the warm cloth. "We were inseparable as kids. But after my mother died, Portia changed."

I looked around, a wave of understanding washing over me. This cottage was the last thing he had of his mother. "I'm sorry," I managed.

"Portia thought our mother had abandoned us. But she didn't. She would never leave us." His expression hardened. "My father killed her and made it look like a suicide."

I blinked at him, startled by his honesty. I couldn't imagine how horrible it must be—truly unthinkable—to know that your father killed your mother. He turned away from me, balling his hands into such tight fists that when he opened them, his palms were dotted with blood.

"But why?" I whispered, unable to stop myself.

"She . . . . found out things about him." He began poking at the fire, the flames jumping out in vicious reds. "I come back here sometimes, to think, and be alone. Portia never does. I'm not sure if she remembers it at all. I'm sorry," he interrupted himself. "I shouldn't be telling you this."

"I'm glad you did." I laid my hand upon his. I recognized a sadness in him, the same sadness I felt. The kind that finds you as a child and sits there forever, never leaving you.

"Did you tell anyone?" I asked quietly.

"No, not even Portia. If my father was put in prison, we would have been all alone. I wanted to spare her from the pain. But . . ." He trailed off, staring into the fire.

"I'm so sorry," I said again. "That must have been a terrible choice."

"You know the strangest part?" His voice sounded bitter. "I still love my father, even knowing what he did. And at the same time I hate him, for who he is, and for what he did to Portia."

I said nothing.

"I grieved for my mother, but it was worse for Portia. She thought our mother didn't love her enough to live for her and take care of her. She went to the barn where she had a family of baby rabbits she'd been taking care of, and broke all their necks. That was the start of the new Portia." He gripped his hands together. "She was eight years old."

I sat in silence, looking into the fire and thinking of my own siblings. I wondered once more where they were buried. Were they with our parents in heaven already? As I thought of all that my family had been through, all the pain and grief and fear, the drive to hurt the man who had done this to us rose up in me once more. "Do you know where Cornelius Hollister is? Do you know where I can find him?"

Wesley looked up at me sharply. "He's in the Tower of London. Why?"

"He killed my mother and father," I said softly, "and probably my brother and sister. He's taken everyone I love from me."

Wesley stared down at his hands, a grim look on his face. "Do you understand how many soldiers are protecting him? How many weapons they have?"

"Yes." I nodded. "I know I'll die in the attempt. I'm prepared for that."

"Don't you understand?" he exclaimed in sudden frustration. "He wants your entire family destroyed! If you die, he can finally crown himself king."

"Isn't that what you want?" I sat upright and took the

cloth away from my cheek. "I haven't forgotten that we're on opposite sides just because you saved my life."

"We aren't on opposite sides," he protested, his voice low.

"As long as you're in Hollister's army, we're on opposite sides."

"I didn't have a choice!"

"There's always a choice." I shook my head. "I understand what it's like to be cold and starving, now, I do. But if you really don't believe in his cause, couldn't you have found another way for you and Portia?"

"That's not it, you don't—" He stopped. "Please just promise me you won't sneak off on some suicidal mission."

My eyes met his, and this time I didn't look away. Instead I let myself study him in the dim firelight. Something had shifted. The hard mask of the soldier had vanished, revealing a sad and lonely boy. I looked at the soft curls of his hair, shining like dark gold, his glittering green eyes, his broad shoulders.

I must look so ugly to him, with my hair cropped close to my skull and the red welt on my cheek. I covered my face with my hands. "Just stop," I said. "I don't—"

"Eliza," he interrupted. He took my hands in his, gently lowering them from my face, lifting my chin to gaze at me in the flickering light. "You are beautiful."

He moved closer to me. I felt his breath on my lips, warm and soft. Then our lips touched. His hand moved tentatively from my cheek to the back of my head, his fingers resting softly in the hollow of my neck, just touching my hairline.

He hesitated for a moment, and I knew that he was giving me a chance to pull away. I answered him by leaning in, opening my mouth to kiss him back, consumed by a strange and restless hunger. In this moment, everything fell away. The brand on my cheek, the sign of the New Guard, the knowledge gnawing at the back of my mind that Cornelius Hollister lived in the Tower of London. All that mattered was that we were here, falling back against the pillows, kissing as the fire turned to embers and slowly grew cold.

Wesley pulled me into his arms, wrapping me in a cocoon of warmth. "It's late," he said. "You should get some sleep. Take the bedroom—I can sleep here." He gestured to the sofa.

I nodded, but didn't want him to let go of me. "Come with me?"

He stood and led me into the bedroom. I lay down under the covers, still in my uniform, pulling him down with me. He placed the lantern on the bedside table, turning the wick low so the room went dark. He wrapped his arms protectively around my waist as he settled in. His skin smelled sweet and fresh, like water. I closed my eyes, pretending for a moment that this could last, that we could always be like this, together in the warmth of this tiny cottage in the middle of a poisoned forest.

19

I SAT UP WITH A START, GASPING FOR BREATH. THE NIGHTMARE was already gone, but fragments lingered, swirling in the dark corners of my mind. Mary and Jamie trapped in a steel cell as men in white coats came to torture them. Me, running madly through a maze, hearing their voices but unable to find them.

It was the middle of the night, and Wesley was still asleep beside me. His head lay on the pillow we shared, his wavy hair falling across his forehead, glowing like fine silver in the moonlight. I leaned forward to kiss his cheek. "Good-bye," I whispered. I felt the sting of sudden tears as I moved away from the bed, desperately hoping he wouldn't wake up, that I would be free to remember him like this.

A few embers still glowed in the fire. I fumbled around in the dark for the candle and lit it on a dying cinder. By the light of the candle, I hurriedly laced up my boots and buttoned the coat of my uniform. The gun was on the round table where I had left it. I tucked it into my pocket.

I looked back through the bedroom door one last time. I was putting Wesley in danger, leaving him here without a horse. But he had his gun to protect him, and he knew these woods well. By the time he woke it would be sunrise and safe enough to walk back to camp. I forced myself to look away and open the front door.

The morning air felt damp and cool. Before I left, I kissed the wall by the door. It was a superstition I had inherited from my grandmother: She always said that if you kissed a door before you left it would ensure a safe return. I hoped, despite all odds, that I could come back here someday with Wesley.

I looked out into the dark, cold night, hoping for at least one star to get my bearings, but there was nothing. Caligula slept standing, a dark shadow against the darker sky, still tethered to the post. I looked fearfully at her huge frame and pulled a handful of wild grass out of the ground.

"Caligula, here, girl," I murmured, holding out the grass and reaching to stroke her nose. At the touch of my hand she reared up, kicking out at me, snorting and baring her teeth. I jumped aside. The chain on her neck rattled as she pulled at it wildly, trying to free herself.

I took a deep breath. I'd been riding horses since I could walk, but I'd never seen a horse like this, raised for destruction. "Shhh," I whispered as I reached out for the reins, pulling them down firmly to look her in the eye.

She paused, and for a moment I thought I'd connected with her. But then she yanked the reins up so quickly that they slipped through my hands, the leather pulling on my bandages and reopening my wounds.

I stared into her dark eyes. Wesley had managed to control her using sheer force, but I lacked the strength. I made low, soothing noises as I reached up and gently slid the halter out from under her ears. She spit out the bit and looked at me with an almost curious expression. "It's just you and me now, Caligula," I murmured. "Can you help me get to London?"

She stood utterly still, blinking at me as I climbed onto her back using the post as a mounting block. Without the reins, I laced my fingers tightly in her mane. I hoped my weight would be enough to direct her. The moment she felt me on her back she took off running, throwing me backward on the saddle.

We hadn't been riding for long when what was left of the sun rose in the east, silhouetting the bare branches of the trees against a brighter patch of gray in the thick darkness. That was all I needed for now. Straightening myself in the saddle, I nudged the warhorse slightly with my left leg, moving her to the right, toward the sliver of gray against the horizon.

Some time later, we trotted up to the edge of a motorway. I pulled Caligula to a stop, squinting into the distance to read the faded, graffitied signs. The gray concrete slab of highway was buckled and broken, the yellow traffic lines faded. This was the motorway to London, but riding on such an open road was not safe. Hollister's forces patrolled the interstate, capturing any lone travelers or refugees from the raided towns.

I tried not to look at the cars scattered across the highway, at the rotting skeletons that sat in the drivers' seats, the smaller bodies of children curled up in the backseats. These people had been driving when the Seventeen Days hit. They had never had a chance.

A rumbling sound came from down the road. I swiftly

slid off Caligula and led her back into the trees, peering out to see what was coming. In the distance, far down the long stretch of highway, a cloud of riders on horseback appeared. Caligula neighed softly, picking up on my fear, and I stroked her coat, shushing her under my breath. There were hundreds of them. The army was a blur of gray on warhorses, the stock horses and diesel trucks behind them. Armed guards sat on top of the trucks, sevils and guns aimed in all directions. As the trucks passed, I heard the horrific screaming of the prisoners inside, banging against the vehicles' metal sides, trying to escape the fate that awaited them in the Death Camps.

When they had passed and the road was empty again, I rested my head for a moment against Caligula's neck, breathing in the warm horsey scent of her. Wesley had rescued me from the Death Camps—I owed him my life. Glimpses of our night together flashed through my mind: the feel of his lips, the warmth of his arms around me, the low sound of his voice. Somehow, the memories already felt far away, but they gave me the strength I needed. They gave me the hope that love still existed in this dark world, that it would exist even after I was gone.

I touched the gun tucked into my belt, checking to make sure it was still secure. The woods were safer than the road;

the best plan would be to ride along the edge near the thinning trees, following the direction of the highway. I let Caligula graze for a moment more, then climbed up onto her back. "To London!" I said. Her ears flicked back for a moment, almost as though she understood me, and then she took off.

Clouds of soot and ash hung like a veil over the city. A thick swarm of pigeons flew overhead. I rode through district NW30, Caligula's hoofbeats echoing hollowly on the deserted streets. From the silence and dark windows, I knew this district had already been invaded by Hollister's army; its people must have been captured and their homes plundered. I stuck to the shadows as we moved past rows and rows of burned-out houses.

Tacked to a boarded-up storefront was a poster of a young brown-haired girl. She sat in a sailor's dress, her hands neatly folded in her lap, her silky hair falling below her shoulders. She had pale skin and rosy cheeks.

WANTED ALIVE

ELIZA WINDSOR

NAME YOUR REWARD

I moved closer to the poster, staring into the girl's bright, hopeful eyes. This picture had been taken a few years ago, in a private sitting for my father; we hadn't distributed royal portraits since my mother's death. My father thought that keeping our faces out of the public eye would keep us safe; and there hadn't been much money for mass printing photographs anyway. I studied the poster. This happy, sheltered person looked nothing like me. They were looking for a girl who no longer existed.

"Help! Somebody, please help!" A woman's high-pitched screams came from a park nearby. I hesitated, wanting to intervene, but desperate to get to the Tower. "Please, no!" she cried, and then, more shrilly, "Help!"

I kicked Caligula, urging her forward and drawing my gun as we approached. I had to at least try.

As I neared, the screaming stopped. A cold, empty silence filled the air. I pulled back on Caligula, reluctant to enter the park. The thought of what could have happened to the woman sickened me. I could have helped her, but I was too late.

Even during the Seventeen Days, London had emergency aid crews to help those in need. Now everything—police, firemen, hospitals—was gone.

I rode on into the night. Finally, the grim turrets of the Tower of London appeared against the skyline. Rising above them all, like a knife slicing open the horizon, stood the Steel Tower. The windowless prison of steel was once protected by an electrical current strong enough to kill anyone on contact. But the current, like every other system that provided order, was gone. As I rode closer I saw a line of Hollister's soldiers guarding the Tower, standing around the moat, sevils at their sides. Somewhere inside was Cornelius Hollister.

We reached the moat surrounding the Tower, and I left Caligula in the dark shelter of an underpass. I had no way to tether her, but I took off her saddle and rubbed her down quickly with a bit of saddlecloth. My nose wrinkled as I caught the brackish stench of the moat's stagnant water. I pulled a few weeds for her and left them in a pile. "Please stay, Caligula," I said. "I need you." I looked into her eyes, willing her not to leave. They were big and brown now, no longer red with rage.

I took a deep breath and pulled the army hat low on my forehead so that my eyes were in shadow. I straightened my uniform, tightening the belt, buttoning the jacket, double-knotting the shoelaces on my boots. I stared down at my reflection in the river water. The burn below my eye shone red and throbbing in the dim light. I ran my fingers along the wall, gathering black soot on my fingertips, rubbing it around the scar, wincing at the pain. Now it looked dirty, dark. More like a bruise.

Now I looked like one of them.

20

DARK CLOUDS OF SOOT SWEPT ACROSS THE CITY SKY, THE DAY-light turning to dusk. The sound of a crank wheel echoed from behind the Tower wall. The drawbridge was being lowered and the guards were changing positions, right on schedule. I crouched down, preparing to run, stretching my aching muscles with a bitter smile.

I had spent the day staking out the Tower and now knew every inch of the grounds, the moat, the wall around it. I had memorized the drawbridge schedule. If I ran quickly I could reach the soldiers about to march inside, joining them and making my way unnoticed to the kitchens. From there, I would follow Hollister's dinner to his chambers. His location might be a secret, even to his followers, but my rumbling stomach reminded me that everyone had to eat.

I took off at a sprint toward the Tower wall, keeping low to the ground and trusting to the gathering dark to hide my movements. I paused for a moment in the shadow of the wall to catch my breath and wipe the sweat off my forehead. Two lines of guards were marching steadily toward the drawbridge. As the last soldier passed, I fell in line behind him, keeping my head low, the rhythm of my feet matching his.

I shivered as we crossed the drawbridge into the Tower. I had always been so afraid of this place, ever since we had come to visit when I was a little girl. The chopping block, the marks in the stone from where the axe had fallen over and over, the bloodstains that still remained after hundreds of years of rain. I thought of the torture chambers where innocent prisoners had suffered—were still suffering. I wondered if they screamed, unheard and unanswered, like the woman in the park. I knew her cries would haunt my nightmares.

Once inside, finding the kitchens was easy. I followed the smell of food and the line of hungry soldiers. Keeping my eyes downcast, I stepped to the back of the line, shuffling forward into a stone entryway. I felt for the gun hidden inside my jacket. In the darkened hallways of the Steel Tower a bell chimed, and a voice rang out from upstairs: "Prisoner feeding time."

The line of soldiers made their way down into a dank dungeon kitchen. Iron pots bubbled over the flames. At the chopping block, a line of cooks severed the heads and tails of rats and mice, sewer snakes and frogs, skinning them and tossing the carcasses into the pots. A cage sat on the floor beside the fire, filled with rats that ran from side to side in a frantic effort to escape their fate.

I glanced across to the other end of the kitchen where a feast was being prepared. Large platters of fruits and cheeses, freshly baked breads, and a tower of chocolate truffles sat on shining silver trays. Bottles of champagne cooled in buckets of ice. I had no idea foods like this even existed anymore. I felt almost dizzy. All I'd eaten today was a handful of weeds and half a stale biscuit I'd found in my jacket pocket. Was all of this for Hollister? I thought of what he had said to me before he killed my father. *Because England is starving, and you are having a ball.* Seeing this feast, I hated him more than ever.

"Stop staring, it'll only make your mouth water," the girl next to me said.

I nodded and looked straight ahead, where an old woman with white hair and bushy white eyebrows stirred the pots with an enormous ladle. "Fill up the bowls! Feeding time for cells one through nine!" she yelled. I nearly gagged as I watched her unlatch the top of the rat cage, lowering her twig-thin arm inside. Quick as pulling an apple from a tree, she plucked out a squirming rat by its tail and tossed it into a bubbling pot, fur and all.

Keeping in step with the soldiers in front of me, I copied their every move, picking up a tray, filling a glass with gray water and a bowl with one ladleful of the rat-and-insect stew. I kept my face expressionless, hard, averting my eyes from the rat foot and mouse head in the bowl on my tray. The soldiers made a line up the stairs. I gripped the tray in my hands, walking shakily behind the girl in front of me.

She paused, glancing to her right and left, looking for a chance to gossip. She put her lips close to my ear. Her breath was sour. "If you want some of the good stuff, talk to me later," she declared self-importantly. "I could help you get some—for a price." She smiled, showing her yellowed teeth.

My eyes darted to the tray in front of her. She wasn't carrying a bowl of stew like the rest of us. Instead, her tray held a pretty pink teacup containing a mix of herbs: rosebuds, lavender, anise, and something else, a yellow flower I couldn't identify.

"That tea smells nice," I said quietly, wondering why her tray was different. Was she the one tasked with serving Hollister?

"It may smell nice, but it's deadly. It's tea for Her Royal Highness." She said the last in a sarcastic singsong, then spat on the stones for emphasis. "The *queen*."

I nearly dropped my tray in shock. Mary was alive.

"They say it makes her weak," the girl went on with a grin. "She's been puttin' up too much of a fight, I hear, but this quiets her real good."

"What if she doesn't drink it?" I asked evenly, trying to disguise the horror in my voice.

"Oh, she drinks it all right. If she don't drink it, the young prince gets whipped," she cackled.

I tried to laugh with her, but all I could manage was a hacking cough. My mind raced as I tried to recover. Jamie and Mary were both alive, and they were here! I would have to come back for Hollister later. I tried to compose my face as I thought of my sister and brother, imprisoned, needing me. I could not wait another second to see them.

I knocked over the gruel on my tray, letting it spill all over the staircase. "Oops!" I exclaimed. "I'm so clumsy."

The girl rolled her eyes. "You'd better clean up that mess before Mrs. Caldwell sees it," she said, turning to continue up the stairs.

I waited a few moments before setting my tray on the ground and trailing the girl up a winding metal staircase. The walls were steel, my reflection a dark, blurry shadow. There were cells on each floor, lined with bars only an inch apart, revealing rows of sickened, dying prisoners. Most of them were whimpering and begging for water. The ones that lay there quietly saddened me even more.

As I tiptoed along behind the girl with the pink teacup, I felt my hatred of Cornelius Hollister gathering inside me like a knot of barbed wire, cutting me from the inside. The spiral staircase continued up and up, soaring high in the narrow tower. Finally, she came to a stop.

I crouched on the floor below and waited until I saw the girl come back down the stairs, her tray now empty. I hovered in the shadows until her footsteps echoed several levels below me. Then I turned and made my way up, my heart beating faster with each step, pausing at the cell door.

Through the narrow gap between the metal bars, I peered inside. Jamie lay on a small cot; Mary sat next to him with her back to me. From behind I wouldn't have recognized her. It was only when I heard her voice gently encouraging Jamie to eat that I knew I was at the right cell. She looked as thin and bony as an old woman. Her shoulders poked through her threadbare, faded red dress. I realized with a start that it was the same one she'd been wearing at the Roses Ball.

She rested Jamie's head in her arm, trying to spoon-feed him. I stood there, blinking back tears, trying to say something, but was unable to make a sound. I glanced around the rest of their cell. There was a small wooden table with a pack of playing cards, a teapot, and a cup. Next to the teapot was a crumpled napkin, stained red.

I pressed my nose into the small space between the bars, watching Mary turn away from Jamie and cover her mouth with her hand—a deep cough racked her whole body. She gradually pushed herself up to stand, pressing her hand against the wall for balance, her other hand still over her mouth. She was moving the way our grandmother moved before she died.

She plucked the red-stained napkin from the table and wiped the blood away from her hand. I could see she was trying to hide it from Jamie.

"Mary, Jamie," I choked out in a gasp.

Mary turned her head to look at me, her expression

hostile, and I realized that she didn't recognize me. I suddenly felt so self-conscious, so embarrassed by my branded face, my butchered hair.

"Mary," I whispered. "It's me, Eliza."

Her eyes lit up, her face brightening with disbelief. "We thought you were dead," she said, her voice hoarse as tears began streaming down her cheeks. I reached out to her, trying to fit my fingers in the space between the bars, but all I could manage was my pinky. Mary squeezed it tight and kissed it.

Jamie came over to the bars, and with the tip of my finger, I managed to touch his cheek. His little body was nothing more than a skeleton. I tried to hide the shock on my face, but I could tell he wasn't doing well. "Have they been giving him his medicine?"

Mary shook her head.

I was surprised he'd lasted this long without it. He stared at me silently, his blue eyes hollow in their sockets.

I pulled the gun out of my jacket. "Mary," I said quickly, "take this gun. The next time the guard delivers your food, kill her. Take her clothes and weapon and escape."

"Eliza." Mary shook her head. "That won't fit through the bars."

I realized in horror that she was right. The single opening, the food slot on the door, was bolted shut, and there was no way to get the gun through the thin slits between the bars.

Mary's worried face watched me as I frantically tried to fit the gun through the gap, hoping that if I turned it just the right way it would fit. "There's no way." She shook her head. "We've tried everything."

"Someone's coming," Jamie said, his eyes wide with worry.

From below came the sound of footsteps echoing against the steel.

"Eliza, run! Hide!" Mary whispered, panicked.

"No! I can't leave you again." I turned around, dropping into a defensive stance, and held the gun out in front of me. If I was going to die, I would do it fighting for my siblings' lives.

"Eliza!" Mary hissed. "Leave! You won't solve anything like this. You can kill those guards but we'll still be trapped in here!"

I ignored her.

Mary summoned herself to her full height. She was always authoritative, but she could be particularly fearsome if she wanted to. "As your queen, I command you!"

I turned to look at her in disbelief. "Mary—" I began.

"There's no time, Eliza," she snapped. "I command you," she said again. "I can't watch you die."

I nodded, my heart so twisted up with love and sadness that it felt like it would burst, and tucked the gun into my pocket. Just then, the guard reached the top of the stairs.

I spun on my heel and tore down the hallway.

"I've got her!" he cried as he took off after me. "This way! She's going this way!"

I turned again and again, lost in a maze of steel passageways and prison cells, hoping I would lose him, but the heavy footsteps followed me at every turn. Each claustrophobic passage looked the same; the walls reflected my image in a blur as I ran onward. Emaciated prisoners stared out at me with eyes demented by torture and the isolation of their cages. The guards' voices multiplied behind me, coming from every direction, resounding off the metal passageways.

And then, the hallway came to a dead end.

I stopped and looked around frantically. I was trapped. I searched the walls with my hands for any way to escape, when I felt a cold wind on my skin. I looked up to see a narrow trapdoor in the ceiling above. It was high, but I had no other choice. I crouched and sprang upward.

I managed to grab the edge of the opening with one hand, but the gun fell out of my grip in the process. I cursed myself for not zipping it back into my jacket. I looked down, wondering if I should go back for it, when I heard footsteps at the end of the hallway.

I swung my other hand up and pulled myself up onto the roof, my arms shaking with the strain. The trapdoor was small, and I barely fit through the opening. One of the steel edges caught my back, scraping through my jacket like a knife. The pain was intense, but I pushed on. If I could barely fit through the opening, it would be too small for a guard to slip through. I had at least a minute until they made it to the roof from the stairs.

"Eliza?"

I whirled around.

Wesley ran to me, holding me close for a moment before pulling back to look in my eyes. How was he here? "I knew you would do something like this. I asked you to promise me." He looked so sad, I ached at having betrayed his trust. "We don't have much time. You need to hide, now!"

I looked around. The rooftop was barren. There was nowhere to hide.

"Wesley, they're alive," I said, my voice breaking. "Please. Help me rescue Mary and Jamie." I had come so close—I couldn't give up now. But he wasn't listening. He was opening

178

the recessed door leading from the floor below to the roof. I heard him shout, "Can't find her up here! Are you sure she's not on level fifty-nine?"

I ducked down, wishing for a crevice or dark corner to hide in, wishing I still had the gun on me. Dozens of guards burst out onto the roof, but my eyes were focused only on one.

"Why, I do believe she's right here," drawled a voice I knew all too well. Cornelius Hollister greeted me with an evil smile, moving toward me with predatory slowness. "Eliza Windsor."

I instinctively took a step backward, blinded by a flashlight that had been directed into my eyes.

"Don't move!" Portia cried. "Or I'll shoot you straight between the eyes. And believe me, I'll enjoy it."

I squinted into the glare. Cornelius Hollister stood across from me, Portia by his side, her gun pointed at me. I dared another step back, away from them, away from the gun. The backs of my knees hit hard against something. A railing.

"Should I kill her?" Portia asked, looking to Hollister.

"No, Portia!" Wesley walked toward her quickly and reached for her weapon. "She's more valuable alive," he continued, his tone rough. "She has secrets we need. Vital information." I searched Wesley's face for some kind of emotion, but he was hidden by shadow.

"Your brother's right," Hollister said. "Thank you for bringing her to me. I would never have recognized her myself, disguised and ugly as she is." Portia laughed loudly at this. Hollister put his arm around Wesley, ruffling his hair affectionately. I gripped the railing behind me as I realized what I was seeing.

Cornelius Hollister was Wesley and Portia's father.

That was what Wesley had been trying to tell me in the cottage when he said he had no choice but to join the New Guard. *Cornelius Hollister* was the father who had murdered their mother because she found out the truth about him. Looking at the three of them now, together, I felt sickened.

I had kissed Wesley. I had trusted him. I might have even, in some deep part of me, felt that I loved him. The son of the man who had killed my parents before my eyes and imprisoned my brother and sister. The enemy.

I felt the railing behind me. I was at the edge of the roof.

Hollister's smile caught the light as he came toward me. From the corner of my eye, I saw the dark water glistening below. I gripped the railing with my right hand, tilting back.

He stood in front of me. "Finally, I have the last one."

His hand reached forward, and I felt his fingertips scrape my skin. I closed my eyes as I jumped backward, hurling myself over the edge.

21

CONCRETE OR KNIFE? THOSE WERE THE WORDS THAT FLASHED through my head as I hurtled down toward the water. As Mary and I had gotten older and more daring with our dives, we'd graduated from the tree branch over the loch to the highest cliffs over the water. The amount of pain depended on the way you landed: in like a knife and you were safe. But if you dove the wrong way, the water could feel as hard as concrete.

I dropped, turning through the air, down the length of the Tower. The water was about ten feet away when I straightened myself out, stretching my arms in front of me, tucking my chin to my neck, bracing myself. But the speed of the fall turned me again, and I landed in the water feet-first, sending me straight to the sludgy bottom of the moat.

The murky water was pitch-black. I couldn't see the surface. I panicked, my lungs burning from lack of air. Something that felt like a wet hand brushed past my cheek and I screamed, or tried to scream, as my mouth filled up with the water. Sewer snakes! I kicked my legs, frantically beating my arms in the water to reach the air.

I gasped as I broke the surface, gulping in breath after breath, like a starving person devouring a plate of food. I swam to the edge of the moat wall, pressing my hands against the stones, feeling for something, anything to hold on to, but the wall was covered in a bright green slime that slipped under my fingers.

I treaded water, kicking frantically and batting away sewer snakes with my arms. An enormous one darted toward me, nipping at my neck. Sewer snakes feed like leeches, clinging to your skin, sucking out the blood. My scream echoed inside the walls of the moat as I flung the snake away.

The drawbridge lowered over the moat and soldiers stormed across it, their guns trained on me. I looked around in panic, still fighting off sewer snakes. The only place to hide was beneath the drawbridge, but it would only be a matter of time before they realized where I had gone.

I would have to give them what they wanted. I flailed my arms, splashing them over my head, and sank down. Then I rose up, gasping for air, then down again. I squeezed my eyes shut as I sank into the muddy bottom and held my breath, waiting. My lungs felt as if they would burst as I let myself drift down toward the bottom, keeping motionless so the surface water would stay still.

Finally, I began to swim carefully toward the rusted iron railing of the drawbridge cranks. Once I was under the bridge, I could come up for air. Still holding my breath, I rose to the surface.

I gripped the steel bar, shivering uncontrollably. Luckily the crowd was so loud they couldn't hear me as I gasped for breath. I was out of sight, safe, but only for a moment. A beam of light crossed the water. The guards' torches.

"Where is she?" a voice shouted. "Did she drown?"

"Crank up the drawbridge!"

I heard the clank of metal as the wheel began to turn. I barely had time to think. My clothes felt like lead and I was sure I was losing blood from the cuts on my back where the trapdoor had scraped me. I felt more exhausted than I'd ever felt before. I was heartsick as I thought of Wesley standing there next to his evil father, of Mary and Jamie, who would probably be killed now because of me. Part of me just wanted to sink to the bottom of the moat. I imagined how peaceful it would feel, even in the filthy water, to be floating, weightless.

But then, in a flash of light, I saw a hole under the shadowy edge of the drawbridge. I stretched my hands toward it, but I slipped. The drawbridge began to lift upward—in a moment they would see me. Gathering the last of my strength, I reached up and pulled myself into the tunnel just as the drawbridge rose.

"Find her! I want her alive!" Hollister's distinctly sinister voice commanded his guards. "Lower the boats, now!"

The searchlights flashed across the water as the guards jumped into rowboats. Where did the tunnel lead? Could I make it to the other side without being discovered?

"She's not here, sir," one of the guards called up. "She must have drowned."

"Set the moat on fire!" Hollister screamed. "That will drive her out!"

The guards began pouring gasoline onto the water, where it floated in slick pools, its noxious smell reaching me in the tunnel. Someone, probably Hollister, dropped a blazing torch from above. The gasoline ignited in a burst of flame like a flower, red tongues racing across the water in all directions.

The tunnel was so narrow that I was forced to inch along on my stomach. The air was thick with smoke. I pulled my shirt up to cover my nose and mouth so I could breathe. I crawled, as fast as I could, away from the smoke and the flames and into the depths of the pitch-black tunnel.

Finally, the darkness in the tunnel began to lift, and I inched the last few feet to its end. I fell onto the street, scraping my hands on the pavement. The air smelled of smoke and I could still hear the voices of the soldiers cheering. I rested my head against the pavement and lay there, too exhausted to move. My cold, wet clothes clung to my body. A burning sensation spread across the wound in my back, but nothing felt as painful as the fact that I was here without my brother and sister.

From my left came the clank of a chain and what sounded like a low growl. I jumped, looking around in the darkness. Two large, shining eyes stared back.

"Caligula?" I asked, unable to believe that she had found me. She nudged me with her nose, hooves pawing the pavement, urging me to get up.

Slowly, my head throbbing, I rose to my feet. I winced as I climbed onto her unsaddled back. To my surprise, she stayed still underneath me. "Please, Caligula, take me home," I said in a broken voice. "Take me to Scotland."

The sound of her hooves beginning to canter across the

pavement comforted me. When I thought we were a safe distance, I looked back over my shoulder. Behind me loomed the Tower, still surrounded by red flames. The screaming crowd of soldiers seemed to glow from the fire rising up from the moat.

I laid a kiss on my tattered fingertips and blew it to Mary and Jamie. "I'll be back for you," I promised, near tears.

22

MY WET CLOTHES FROZE AGAINST MY SKIN AND I SHIVERED. MY back throbbed with pain. The street faded in and out of focus. I tried to picture the road map of Scotland that had hung in my father's study. It had been there my whole life, but all I could remember were winding lines and the ornate brown frame.

I looked up in the sky for the North Star. There it was, right where it had always been. It was comforting to think that even though the world had changed so much, the stars were still the same. If I used the sky as my guide, hopefully I would find my way to the old motorway and then on to Scotland. "It's going to be a long ride," I said to Caligula, patting her neck.

As we moved through the streets, the wind blew bits of trash toward us—a broken umbrella spiraling dangerously, dirty scraps of paper. Ash stung my eyes. Caligula charged out of the city on the crumbling, cracking motorways, past the freestanding homes in the London suburbs, the desolate gray shopping malls and parking lots like graveyards filled with rusting cars and their long-dead owners.

A faded highway sign read SCOTLAND: 380 MILES. Streams of warm tears fell from my eyes and the stars streaked overhead in a blur. I kept replaying the events of the night over and over. I couldn't believe I had found Mary and Jamie, only to fail them. I couldn't believe that the man I'd been fantasizing about killing was Wesley's father. My head swam thinking about it, and I blinked into the cold night as the wind whipped around me.

The cold set into my bones and I began shaking so violently that I couldn't keep myself upright. I nudged Caligula toward the forest on the side of the road. I needed to rest.

My legs were so shaky that when I slid off the tall horse, I collapsed into a heap on the cold ground. Spots danced before my eyes. I couldn't tell how far we were from the interstate, but said a silent prayer that it was far enough. I curled up in a pile of twigs and mulch, fumbling to pull the frozen New Guard jacket off me. It was so wet that it would do more

189

harm than good. I tried to warm my frozen fingers with my breath. Caligula lowered her front legs and lay down next to me. I nestled into her, grateful for her body heat. Finally, mercifully, I drifted off to sleep.

My eyes shot open. Something was moving through the branches.

I listened carefully, suddenly wide awake. I wasn't sure how long I had slept, but the sky was still black overhead.

I lay motionless, waiting for whatever it was to take another step. I had spent enough time in the Scottish woods to recognize the sounds of certain creatures. A mouse or squirrel moved quickly, darting from hiding place to hiding place. Once I sat below a tree with Bella and watched a brown bear make its lazy way across the forest floor, its footsteps slow and booming. But these footsteps were not delicate like a fox or lumbering like a bear. They were unmistakably human.

I tucked myself under Caligula, her giant body rising and falling with each breath. The crunching sound of footsteps was only a few yards away.

"I smell a horse," a man said.

"I smell human." The second man's voice was ragged, deeper than the first.

I lay still, barely breathing. If I was quiet enough, maybe they would move on.

The footsteps drew closer. I felt Caligula's heartbeat begin to race, but she remained still, sensing my fear.

I heard them move farther away and risked looking up from behind Caligula, trying to determine where they were. Without making a sound, I rolled onto my side.

There was silence in the woods. I let out a breath of relief.

"This is my kill!" the gravelly voice suddenly shouted above me. I looked up to see a man standing over me, holding up an axe. I screamed, frozen with fear, unable to take my eyes from the gleaming blade.

Just as he began to lower the axe, Caligula jumped up, letting out a giant roar, so loud it could have come from a pride of lions.

"What the hell?" The man stumbled back in fear, dropping the axe to the ground. Caligula charged at him, throwing him forcefully back against a tree with her head. His neck jerked at an unnatural angle and his limp body fell to the ground. I watched, stunned. I had never seen a warhorse in full attack mode before.

From out of the darkness, the second man lunged at me.

His wild eyes flashed as he opened his mouth, revealing a set of metal nails drilled into his gums instead of teeth. Nails for chewing human flesh. I reached out for the fallen axe and hurled it into his body without thinking twice.

The blade caught him in his side, and his filthy body slumped heavily against mine. A puddle of warm blood oozed from his chest onto my shoulder. I pushed him off me and stood for a moment in shock, staring at his body.

"Caligula," I called, taking an unsteady step forward. There was no sign of her. I slumped back against the tree, lacking the strength even to think of where to go from here.

Then I heard her hooves, racing through the trees in my direction. "Good girl," I murmured as she approached.

I climbed up onto Caligula's back, knowing there would be no more sleep for me tonight, and we flew off.

23

WE REACHED A SMALL, QUIET VILLAGE JUST AS THE SKY BEGAN to turn a lighter shade of gray. I pulled back gently on Caligula's mane, slowing her to a walk as I took in the row of small shops: a bakery, a tailor, a general store. A white wooden church with its bell tower pointed toward the sky like praying hands. The town was an oasis, seemingly untouched by Cornelius Hollister's destruction.

The streets were silent, the windows of the thatch-roofed houses dark. With the villagers still asleep, I felt safe leading Caligula up to a well on a hill overlooking the village center. I lowered the bucket and pulled up a pail of fresh water. I was thirsty, but I let Caligula drink first.

She had been running for hours and her coat was damp with sweat.

When she finished, I drew a second bucket of water for myself, drinking greedily. It tasted so pure. I sank to the ground, my legs shaky from the effort of riding for so many hours. The wounds on my back throbbed and red marks ran up my arms. I twisted around, pulling up my shirt to try to see the source of the pain, and gasped. A deep gash ran the length of my spine. Remembering Wesley's instructions to clean any wound before it grew infected, I dipped the pail once more and let the cool water rinse my cuts. It would need more care, but I knew that Polly's mother would have an ointment if I could just make it to Balmoral.

I thought back to the first time I met Polly. Mary and I had been walking down the lane, looking for blackberries, when we saw a thin, grubby-looking girl coming toward us. In her arms were two overflowing baskets full of the plump berries.

"Where did you get those?" Mary asked, and I could tell she was worried the girl had left nothing behind for us.

"I found them," Polly replied with an infectious smile, revealing a gap between her two front teeth. She had straight reddish-brown hair, round green eyes, and a splattering of freckles across her nose.

"Well, my father owns all these lands, so technically they belong to us," Mary said, using her most clipped upper-class voice.

The girl's face fell as she stared sadly at the baskets in her arms. "My mum was going to make jam."

"Don't worry," I said quickly, with a sharp look at Mary. "You can keep them, if you just show us where you found them."

She led us to a secret place. We followed her under the branches of low-growing apple trees, wading through an ice-cold stream, until Polly pulled back the thorny branches to reveal a grove of perfectly ripe blackberries.

We spent the afternoon picking them, tasting a few here and there. Then we followed her back to her cottage, where her mother showed us how to make the berries into jam. From then on, we spent the rest of our summers together, and during the school year we kept in touch by sending each other weekly letters and occasionally small packages. Those memories seemed a million years away.

Watery sunlight spilled through a crack in the clouds, illuminating the town below and rousing me from my memory. One by one the windows of the houses lit up with lanterns. Two men pushed a cart of goods toward the market square. As comforting as it felt to be in a village untouched by Hollister, I was losing strength, and my scrape needed to be treated. "Ready, Caligula?"

She looked up from the empty bucket and walked toward me. I tried to climb onto her back but couldn't even pull myself up. I upended the empty water bucket and used it as a step to help me hoist myself up. As I moved, the pain in my back spread to my chest and ribs. I tried to push it from my mind.

Caligula trotted slowly and steadily up the road leading out of the village and into the hills, past barren fields and skeletal trees. I heard the sounds of birds all around us, but they weren't the same birds I had grown up with. Mockingbirds, blue jays, and sparrows were long gone. The streets had been littered with their bodies for months after the Seventeen Days. Only the carrion birds survived: the crows and pigeons and vultures.

We continued on for hours, each bump in the road sending hot pain through my back. Finally, I recognized a bend in the road. We were just a mile or two away. Soon I would see the square stone house with dark green shutters where Polly and her family lived. I pictured their dogs, lounging on the steps in the front yard, where her mother planted roses and daffodils.

"It's just up here!" I called out, and Caligula, catching

my enthusiasm, hurried forward. My eyes searched the hill-side eagerly, but all that remained in the place where Polly's house had been was the square foundation, charred black by flames, and the ash-covered brick chimney.

I was too stunned to cry, too stunned to feel anything except a hollowing emptiness. I knew the truth instantly. The New Guard had come here looking for me and had killed Polly and her family. Three more people, people I had loved dearly, had lost their lives because of me.

Balmoral Castle still stood up ahead, its walls scorched and covered in soot.

Memories flooded my mind: Mary and me as children, rushing outside in our summer dresses to greet our mother and father. Playing a game of tag in the cavernous hallways. Fishing in the stream with Polly and her father. I closed my eyes, trying to block them out. How could our lives have turned out this way? How could they have changed so suddenly?

I needed to see the stables even though I dreaded what I would find there. I braced myself for the worst but somehow found the strength to urge Caligula forward, walking through the high grass, past the length of the castle, then down a narrower muddy lane to the stables. I looked through the stable windows as we passed. There were no horses inside, and the fields were empty too. Were they stolen, or had they been lucky enough to run away?

"Jasper," I called, trying unsuccessfully to whistle. I took a breath and tried again, looking out into the fields and willing Jasper to appear, cantering toward my call. I stared until the grass and sky blurred together. There was no Jasper. There was no Polly.

There was nothing left.

I dismounted heavily and let Caligula graze in the field. "You're free now," I whispered. She lifted her head, her wide eyes meeting mine, and nudged me lightly with her nose. "No one will ever put a spiked bit in your mouth again. These fields are all yours. You can run forever." I pressed my forehead to hers. "I hope you have a better life here."

My hand fell from her neck and I turned away from her to walk slowly toward the castle. The muddy trail turned into a slate path, which ended in the wide steps leading to the double wooden doors of the front entrance. The doors were closed.

Looking back one last time, I saw that Caligula had followed and was watching me from the path.

"Go!" I was surprised to feel that my face was wet with

tears. I waved my hand in the air, but she just stood there, staring at me.

The air inside the stone hallway was freezing cold. Shards of broken glass covered the floor, sparkling like ice in the dim light that filtered in through the windows. The grand chandelier that had hung in the castle entranceway for centuries lay on the marble floor, shattered into a million pieces. The royal portraits on the walls had been slashed at the throat, my ancestors beheaded. The vases, the art, the mirrors, the paintings—all shattered and destroyed. At least the beautiful old staircase was still standing, though it, too, was scarred with burn marks.

I wanted to check the whole house to see if anything remained, but I was shaking and feverish. A wave of heat would blaze through me, only to leave me feeling ice cold. My limbs felt heavy as I gripped the banister, pulling myself painfully up the stairs. It felt like someone was raking a weapon down my back, and I thought of what the girls had done to Vashti.

I gripped the charred railing to steady myself. All I wanted was to lie down in my room, on my bed. That was the single thought occupying my fevered brain. And so I kept going, step by step. The floor seemed to be rising and falling, disorienting me. I felt like a ship on rough seas.

By the time I made it to my doorway, I was on all fours. The wardrobe had been pushed over, the dark wood splintered on the carpet, and the bedsheets had been flung to the floor. But Bella's round dog bed was in the corner, still indented with her shape, and my own four-poster bed was mostly intact. Even after everything that had happened, this room felt like home. Unlike my mother and father, who were nothing but memories now, this space, this house, would go on, outliving all of us. Maybe someday another girl would wear my dresses and open the jewelry box I'd had since I was six and see the ballerina inside turn.

My head suddenly felt too heavy to hold up. I leaned back and let it hit the wooden floor as I lay there, staring at my bed, wishing I had the energy to walk to it. In the light from the upper windows, I could see the wounds along my arm more clearly. Streaks of red bubbled like a blister, spreading in a line. Infection. I closed my eyes as I drifted into a fitful sleep, full of fiery nightmares.

I woke up, and in my delirious state, I thought I heard voices in the hallway, the sound of footsteps. The door of the room creaked open. I didn't know how Cornelius Hollister had found me already, but in that moment I welcomed death. I lay there, unable to move, my eyes closed.

"Eliza, is that you?"

My eyes opened and took in the face of the person standing over me. The long straight hair, the smattering of freckles, the round, green eyes wide with surprise.

"Polly," I breathed.

24

I FLOATED IN AND OUT OF CONSCIOUSNESS, HOT WITH FEVER. Someone had carried me to my bed and was feeding me spoonfuls of water. At first I thought Polly and I were dancing in the rain, sticking out our tongues to catch the fat droplets. Then I saw her face hovering above me, frowning with concern, and I remembered.

There was a woman, too, with a soft voice and gentle hands. She held my head on her lap, trying to feed me broth, but I was unable to swallow. A man came, dressed in a dark coat and carrying a small case of medicines. He sat down on the bed beside me and took my temperature under my arm, the way my mother had when I was a girl.

"One hundred and six." His voice was grave. "We need an antibiotic to fight the infection."

"Should we move her?" Polly asked, her voice full of worry.

"She's too ill to move," the doctor said.

A group gathered around him talking in low, solemn voices. With the New Guard taking over the pharmacies and hospitals, the doctor was unable to get the medicine he needed for my condition. I saw Polly run from the room, and then I blacked out.

The delirium was a welcome escape. My mind flooded with my happiest memories, so vivid I could actually hear my mother's voice and smell the scent of her rose oil. I felt Bella's soft fur, the cold wet touch of her nose. But when the trembling came back, so did the nightmares: Mary, a skeleton behind bars, Jamie dying alone on a prison cot, the stillness in my father's eyes as he bled to death on the ballroom floor.

I woke up screaming.

"Eliza, it's all right," Polly was saying as she held a damp cloth to my forehead. The room came into focus and I lay back down on the pillow, the sound of my heart pounding in my ears.

"What did the doctor say?" I asked.

When she didn't answer, I knew they hadn't found any antibiotics. "We're doing everything we can. I went to the market this morning." I could tell by the tone of Polly's voice that she was beginning to cry. "Mr. Seabrook, the old chemist, said he might know where to get some. I'll go back tomorrow morning. Mum's in the village knocking on doors, asking if anyone has any left over in their medicine cabinets."

I nodded, but even the slightest movement hurt my head. No one would have any medicine left over. "Hollister's taken over the hospitals?"

"Yes." Polly nodded solemnly. "There were even some of his soldiers in the market square this morning. One of them was following me."

"We can't fight them," I managed, my voice breaking. "They have guns and ammunition. . . ." Then the shivers began again and I lay back down, unable to force a word between my chattering teeth.

Polly looked at me, fighting to conceal her worry, her small nose wrinkling up like it always did before she cried. She pulled the covers to my chin and lay down next to me, wrapping her arms around me to keep me warm.

The door creaked open and the doctor appeared. "She

needs to rest, Polly," he gently rebuked her, and she sat up and moved away.

He walked toward me, carrying the amber-colored bottle of medicine that stopped my shivers and made me sleep. I felt his hands holding my jaw open and pouring the astringent syrup down my throat. A heaviness spread over me like a blanket. I tried desperately to call Polly's name, but blackness overcame me.

When I woke up, Polly's parents and the doctor were sitting on chairs at my bedside. Clara held my hand in hers, squeezing softly like my mother used to. She smiled sadly at me, her eyes red from crying.

"How do you feel, Eliza?" the doctor asked.

I tried to answer, but I could barely open my mouth. I panicked and looked from the doctor to Clara, then to George, who sat with his hands clasped in front of him, staring down at the floor.

"Tetanus causes your jaw to lock," the doctor explained when I tried again to speak.

"I'm so sorry, Eliza," Clara said, leaning close to me. "We can't find any medicine. We've looked everywhere and asked everyone. George rode out for days to all the surrounding towns and villages, but no one has any left."

Tears welled up in her eyes as she spoke. I knew without her saying another word that they had all come to tell me I was dying.

"The infection has spread," the doctor said.

I would have laughed if I'd been able to open my jaw. I had leapt from the roof of the Steel Tower, fended off sewer snakes, crawled through a tunnel chased by fire, and ridden more than three hundred miles bareback. And yet it was a rusty metal trapdoor infected with tetanus that would be the death of me.

"Bury me next to my mum," I tried to say. I wanted to be wrapped in muslin and placed in the ground next to my mother. I imagined our bones touching in the dirt, as close as we would come to holding hands again.

I closed my eyes, bracing myself for another round of shivers. The sleeping syrup the doctor had given me eased the pain, but it left me unable to eat, and I could feel my bones against the mattress. A ray of sunlight shone through the eyelet curtains that had been in my room since I was a child.

"Maybe she's thirsty," Clara said as she settled behind me on the bed, resting my head in her arms. She spoon-fed me, alternating between water and chamomile tea. I felt the tea drip down my throat into my empty stomach.

"It's a beautiful day," I said as clearly as possible, but my words were garbled and sounded like mumbles. Clara understood me.

"It is a beautiful day," she agreed.

Clara left the window ajar as they left the room, allowing the cool air to seep in. It almost smelled like the ocean, damp from the dew but crisped by the sun. I breathed it in slowly through my nose. I had been breathing the air my whole life, but only now did I appreciate how sweet it was. Perhaps it was the delirium, but I could even make out the faint aroma of flowers. It made me think of the pattern of roses on the sofa in Wesley's cottage, where we had sat and kissed in the dancing firelight. As suddenly as that image flashed in my mind, I tried to push it away; I did not want to spend my last few hours thinking about him.

I drifted off, half-dreaming, half-praying for Mary and Jamie. I hoped their death at Hollister's hands would be as painless and swift as possible. I prayed that Polly and her family would never suffer for having helped me. And even now I prayed that someone would kill Hollister, or that a giant sunball would fall on him and his army, burning them all. I couldn't die peacefully knowing that he was still alive.

Some time later, I felt Polly's cool hand on my forehead. "It's okay, Eliza," she murmured.

"Polly, you've been the best friend in the world." I forced the words through my locked mouth. "I love you so much." I closed my eyes, content with my last good-bye.

25

I COULDN'T SLEEP. SHAKEN FROM CHILLS AND FEVER, I LAY IN bed, my eyes open but unseeing. The streaks of gray light at the bottom of the window meant I had survived to see another day.

A loud pounding resounded through the house.

Polly was lying next to me, her arm draped over my waist. She shot up and looked around the room. Her mother, who had nodded off in an armchair in the corner, snapped awake in panic.

"Who would be at the door at this time of night?" she said fearfully.

She moved the curtain back from the window, pushing it

open to peer outside. "Hello? Who's there?" she called out into the night. "Hello?" There was no reply, only the sound of horses' hooves echoing down the stone path, becoming fainter and fainter.

"I'd better go downstairs and look," George said. His voice sounded tired, beaten down.

"I'll come with you," Polly offered, but I squeezed her hand in mine. I wanted her to stay. I was afraid to be alone, to die alone. Polly understood and lay back down beside me.

A few minutes later, George burst back in. "Someone's left this package outside the door," he said breathlessly, holding it out in front of him.

"What is it?" Clara asked, taking the candle from my bedside table to examine the package. It was a small bundle, wrapped in brown paper and tied with string. I could hear the rustling of paper being unwrapped, then silence as she held the contents up to the flickering candlelight. I opened my eyes, straining to see. In her hands she held what looked like a glass vial.

"What does it say, Mum?" Polly asked eagerly.

"Penicillin . . . take three times a day for four weeks."

"Medicine?" Polly asked excitedly. "It's medicine! One of the townspeople must have found some."

"Did they leave a note?" Clara asked.·

Polly looked inside the package. "No."

Clara looked puzzled. "Maybe it was Mr. Seabrook? He was trying to find some this morning."

"Let's not worry right now about where it came from," George said urgently. "We need to hurry and crush the pills so we can mix them in milk. Otherwise she won't be able to swallow them."

Polly sat down beside me, lifting me upright as her dad spoon-fed the bitter-tasting milk into my mouth. After days without eating, even the milk felt hard to swallow. Polly saw me struggling and paused to dribble some water in my mouth, which helped a little.

"Antibiotics have a short shelf life," George said as he poured more milk into the spoon. "Let's just pray it's not too late for the medicine to work."

At first, the doctor checked on me three times a day, giving me the pills at dawn, noon, and evening. Every time he took my temperature, a smile formed on his otherwise stern face. The tremors abated and so did the sweats, and eventually the muscles in my mouth loosened so I could speak again. The red lines of infection spreading to my heart slowly receded until the only evidence left of them were faint scars along my arms and back.

When my fever had been gone for a week straight, the doctor started coming every other day to make sure I was eating. He said I had lost close to a quarter of my body weight. My muscles were still so weak that I wasn't allowed to walk alone in case I fell.

Polly was constantly at my side. She brought me trays of food, porridge with honey that her father had gathered from the honeybee hive, and cream from their dairy cow. At lunch she'd make a broth with whatever she could find, a carrot or potato, and serve it with a small dish of blackberries. I still didn't have much of an appetite but I forced myself to eat for Polly's sake. She looked happy every time I returned an empty dish to her. And slowly, in bits and pieces, I began to tell Polly what had happened since I had said good-bye to her last summer. I had yet to tell her about Wesley—those memories were still too painful. I wondered if I ever would.

"It's the worst feeling in the world, Polly," I said. I was feeling much better physically, but I couldn't stop replaying that night in the Tower. "I was so close to them—our hands touched through the bars of the cell—but then I had to leave them. Sometimes I think I should have just stayed. Then at least we would all have been killed together. . . ."

"No, Eliza!" Polly said fiercely. "Stop talking like that. You tried your best to save them, and we're going to try again."

"It's too dangerous," I began, shaking my head, but she cut me off.

"Resistance forces have been gathering here for a while. They're not enormous, but their numbers are growing every day. Not everyone believes what Cornelius Hollister says." Polly paused, and her voice grew small. "The night his troops burned down our house, he was here, pouring gasoline right alongside them. Luckily we'd been warned by the village watchman and escaped before they arrived."

"And they haven't been back since?" I asked.

"No—not yet, anyway."

"Well, I'm sure they'll come back soon, especially if they find out I'm here."

Polly nodded. "That's why we have to make sure they don't find out."

"Do the Resistance troops have guns? Ammunition?"

Polly shook her head. "We have a little, but we need more. Ammunition is low. But the important thing is that people are banding together. The blacksmith in town is making swords and bludgeons based on old medieval models . . . people are trying whatever they can."

"The New Guard have guns and sevils, stores of ammunition, warhorses and uniforms," I said weakly. "I don't know how we'll stand a chance against them." Her face fell. I didn't want to destroy her hopes, but she needed to know what the Resistance forces were up against. "Our biggest problem is the sheer size of the army. You know he raids districts and takes prisoners, but he also forces the men and women to fight for him. If they refuse he sends them to the Death Camps, where they work until they're no longer useful. And then . . ." I thought back to what I'd seen that awful night and shuddered. "They're forced to dig their own graves and then executed."

Polly looked terrified. "You need to rest," she said quickly. "All this talk of Death Camps isn't helping you get better."

I leaned back onto the pillows as she tiptoed quietly out the door. She was right; I needed to focus on regaining my strength. The early evening light filtered through the windowpanes, laying a lavender shadow across the bed. I knew I should be grateful that I was alive, but there was such a feeling of heaviness inside me now. So many things had gone wrong; everything I had tried to do had failed. I stared up at the cracked ceiling. When I was younger I would gaze at the snaking lines and imagine a rabbit, a moon, houses, trees. But now I only saw cracks.

26

IT HAD BEEN A FEW WEEKS SINCE WE RECEIVED THE MYSTERIOUS donation of penicillin and I was finally starting to feel like myself. In some ways, it seemed like this was just another summer: Polly and I spent the days together while I tried to regain my strength. We took walks around the grounds and read by the fire at night. But all my waking thoughts kept returning to Mary and Jamie imprisoned in the Tower. I hoped they were still alive and not in pain.

One morning we came downstairs to find Clara and George at the breakfast table, drinking their morning tea and eating warmed-up pieces of brown bread spread with a few mashed raspberries. Clara was chopping a mixture of tired-looking carrots and potatoes, tossing them into a large pot for a stew. "How can we expect the troops to survive on this?" she asked in dismay.

George shook his head, not even bothering to look up from the antique hunting rifle he was attempting to repair. It used to hang on the wall of my father's office as decoration; seeing it now filled me with a deep sadness. I missed him so much.

I sat down by the fire while Polly put on water for tea. I looked around, taking in the stacks of dishes, the empty sacks of flour and sugar, the barren cupboards. The kitchen had always been my favorite part of the castle. It was so cozy; no matter the time of year, there was always a fire roaring down here. I used to think that if the castle were a body, the kitchen would be its heart.

"How are you feeling today?" Clara asked me carefully.

"Better, I think." The fire felt nice against my back. I rolled my shoulders and stretched my neck. My muscles were still weak, but they no longer ached.

Clara looked up, catching her husband's eye, and nodded to him.

"Eliza," George said, laying down the pin and wrench he used to repair the rifle. "We need to talk to you."

"We've been waiting till you were feeling better," Clara

interrupted. Her eyes shifted hesitantly to her husband and then back to me. "It breaks my heart to say this, but we don't think it's safe for you to be here with us anymore. We've been looking for a family for you to stay with, where we think you'll be safe."

"A family to stay with?" I repeated, feeling a heavy pit in my stomach.

"Mr. and Mrs. Keats in Wales. They're old friends of your father's—you may remember them from when you were little. They used to visit your family in London."

"I'm leaving? You're sending me to Wales?" I looked from Clara to George. "Please," I begged. "This is my home. It's all I have left from my past."

Clara shook her head. "Eliza, I know this is hard, but it's the best way to keep you safe right now. If Cornelius Hollister captures you and kills you, the Windsor line will be dead, and then he'll declare himself king. We can't let that happen."

My heart skipped a beat as I realized what she was implying. "Are you saying . . ." I swallowed. "Are Mary and Jamie already dead?"

"No, no—we haven't had any news. Until we hear the worst, we need to assume the best. I'm sure they're still alive. But we need to keep you safe." Clara smiled and squeezed my shoulders in support, but I knew she was telling me what

I wanted to hear rather than the truth. "General Wallace is going to escort you to Wales with troops from the Resistance forces as extra protection."

"I can't just run away and hide," I protested, as a tear slid down my nose and onto the wooden table. "I've already lost so much. This place is my only link to the past."

"You have your life!" George exclaimed. "And that's what we are trying to protect." He paused, speaking more gently now. "Your father was a good man. He treated us well—like family. I promised him I would do whatever I could to protect you, and that's what I'm doing now."

Clara reached for my hand. "It's not safe for you to stay here anymore, Eliza, and it's not safe for us to harbor you. They will come back, looking for you."

I nodded; of course she was right. If the New Guard found me here, Polly and her family would certainly be killed. I couldn't let them risk their lives for me. "When do I have to leave?"

A silence fell between Clara and George as they looked at each other. Finally George said, "General Wallace will take you tonight after dusk. We think it's safest if you travel in the dark."

"Tonight," I repeated dully. "Okay. You're right, it's for the best."

Polly put her arm around me, but it only made me feel worse. I forced myself to drink the tea and finish my piece of toasted bread, thinking how hard it would be to say good-bye to her again. Would I ever be able to come back to the places I knew and the people I loved? Or would I be in exile forever?

When I finished, I stood up and carried my mug to the bucket of washing water. "I'm going upstairs to pack up some things for the journey."

"I'll come with you," Polly said, getting up from the table.

"I think I just want to be alone for a while, if that's okay."

As I headed up the stairs, I found myself thinking of when Mary and I were younger and used to pick dandelions on the hill. We would blow the seeds into the wind and watch them float away. I thought of my family, disappearing like the seeds. Now I would be the next to go.

The stone floors echoed beneath me as I took one last walk through the castle, saying my silent good-bye to each of the rooms. I said good-bye to the eggshell-blue living room with the marble mantelpiece where we used to hang our Christmas stockings. I said good-bye to the nursery, where we first realized just how sick Jamie would always be.

I said good-bye to the dark wood-paneled gentlemen's smoking room, and the formal ballroom, and the ladies' tea room with its white molding that always made me think of a wedding cake. And finally, I made my way to my father's study.

As I opened the door, the dust was visible in shafts of sunlight that fell through the windows onto the thick oriental rugs on the floor. My father's desk sat in its usual place, the chair pushed back as though he had only recently gotten up to leave.

My father had loved antiques. A collection of small racing cars, a leather camera next to a sealed box of film rolls, a collection of old cassette tapes and mobile phones and a collection of metal toy soldiers. Mary and I used to make fun of him, rolling our eyes and calling him old-fashioned.

The smell in the room was a mixture of old stone, tobacco, and wood, a scent I would forever associate with my father. My eyes burned. I had never been here without him. I wondered if he was watching over me now, if he knew how much I missed him and needed him.

I kissed the wall of his office and made my way up the stairs. There was still a lingering draft, drifting down the hallways.

• • •

"Eliza?" Polly stood in the doorway of my bedroom. I wasn't even packing, just staring aimlessly out the window. "The sun came out," she said uncertainly. "Do you want to go outside? It might make you feel better."

I touched the window ledge, looking down at the chipping paint. "All right."

Outside, the sun warmed the muddy lanes. We walked slowly, without speaking, down a path that used to be a car road. We passed the remains of the apple orchard, with its trees that stood bare and empty, their branches outlined against the sky like skeletons. Even though there hadn't been apples since before the Seventeen Days, their scent lingered like a stubborn ghost.

"Polly," I breathed, stopping in my tracks. Growing in a patch of dirt by the side of the road was a sapling. I bent down, examining the new growth more closely. A delicate, smooth trunk, sprouting two thin branches, where small almond-shaped leaves were forming.

Polly crouched down beside me with a look of amazement on her face. I felt tears spring into my eyes. Tears of hope.

After the Seventeen Days, so many plant species had died out for good. It hit my mother the hardest—she'd always had a special love for green, growing things. The day she died, during our picnic in the garden, she had said, "I hope that someday, during your lifetime, green leaves come back to the world." It was one of the last things she ever said to me.

I smiled for a moment, happy that my mother had gotten her wish. But then I thought of Mary and Jamie and my smile vanished. They would probably never get to see the new leaves. As if sensing my thoughts, Polly reached out and grabbed my hand, squeezing it.

Just then we heard a strange sound in the distance. It was like the rumble of car tires, except no one here had any oil to drive a car. Polly and I froze, staring at each other in fear.

The rumbling grew louder, closer. It wasn't a truck, I realized, as a group of horses rounded the bend up ahead. It was a squadron of Hollister's soldiers.

We stared in disbelief at the seemingly endless trail of men and women in uniform, sevils at their sides, riding up the winding country roads. They looked like a giant green snake, moving together in perfect unison. These weren't the new recruits I'd seen at the training camp—this was a real army, with horses, new weapons, and clean uniforms. The color in Polly's face drained.

"They'll crush the Resistance forces in one second flat,"

she said, still staring ahead, her expression a mixture of fear and awe.

Before I knew what was happening, Polly jumped in front of me and pushed me backward into a briar patch. I stumbled into the bushes, the twigs and close-knit branches making it nearly impossible to move. I thought Polly would jump in after me, but she just stood by the side of the road, looking forward as though nothing had happened. Three of the riders had broken off from the rest and were headed toward us.

"Polly, come here," I whispered, but she gestured for me to be quiet. The horses were approaching. I sank back into the hollow space beneath the lowest branches, squeezing them so tightly my knuckles turned white. *Please don't hurt her, please don't hurt her*, I prayed. Maybe they would ride right past her, thinking she was just a village girl on her way home.

The sound of the horses grew slower, and I knew the soldiers weren't going to ride on past. I couldn't see their faces, only the muscular legs of the warhorses as they stomped their spiked metal hooves. Polly stood still. I could only see her thin legs and the back of her shorts, and her hand shaking nervously, holding a bunch of twigs behind her back.

"Do you live here?" I heard one of the riders ask.

"Yes," Polly replied meekly. "I live up the road in Balmoral. I was just gathering sticks for the cooking fire."

"Speak loudly and clearly when we address you, girl!" a second soldier snapped. "Do you have any information on Princess Eliza's whereabouts?"

Polly was silent.

"Answer us now!" the angry soldier shouted, raising his sevil. Quickly and without warning, he swung it, slapping her across the face with the flat of the blade. Polly fell backward from the force of the blow and landed on the ground a few feet in front of me. She sat there, pressing her hand to her face and staring up at them, still saying nothing.

"That's enough," ordered another soldier. My breath caught at the sound of his voice. He spoke much more gently. "Now have you seen or heard any information concerning Eliza Windsor?"

It was all I could do not to step out and look at Wesley. I wanted to see his face one last time in the daylight and ask him why he hadn't told me the truth about who he was. Ask him why he had stood there on that roof next to his father when he could have been standing next to me.

Polly pushed herself up. From where I watched, I saw the palms of her hands were bloodied and scraped from the fall.

"If you can provide us with any tips that result in finding

her, you will be compensated by Cornelius Hollister with money or food, whichever you prefer," Wesley said.

Polly nodded.

"Was that a yes?" the first soldier asked sternly.

"Yes," Polly said quietly.

"Yes, you know where the princess is?" the rider repeated. His horse moved and he yanked on the reins to still him. "Tell us! We haven't got all day."

Polly's hand shook nervously as she stammered, "Eliza Windsor, the Princess of England . . ."

I sat up, about to push apart the branches and surrender myself.

". . . is buried next to her mother in the Royal Cemetery in London."

A shocked silence fell among the riders. The only sound was the restless jingle of the horses' bridles as they shifted their weight.

"She's dead?" the soldier said, as though disappointed by the idea. "We wanted her alive. How do you know? Are you sure?"

"Yes," Polly murmured, looking down. "She died of infection from tetanus and fever. They found her body on the road to Balmoral. I guess she wanted to come here to die. My father is one of the men who helped carry her body to

London for burial. He said she was all skin and bones, almost unrecognizable," she finished, her voice low and sad.

The horses pawed the ground anxiously, sending up dust from the road. I could hear the riders talking among themselves, but Wesley remained silent.

"Well, no need to continue on this way, then," he said finally, his tone flat. "We've already taken everything worthwhile from the castle, so let's just head back to Division Eight for the Newcastle raid."

I heard the horses turning and the sound of hoofbeats receding in the distance, heading toward the Northern Road.

"Polly!" I scrambled out of the branches and ran to throw my arms around her. "Thank you! That was so brave of you. You saved me." I stared at the red mark across her face where the soldier had struck her. Her face was pale, and I could see she was shaken.

We sat on the stone wall for a minute to gather ourselves. "That soldier, the one with the blond hair," I began, absently running a finger over the thin scar on my arm, trying to make my voice sound casual. "Did he seem . . . upset, when you said I died?"

Polly looked up at me strangely. "Eliza," she said, speaking slowly, "he was here to capture you."

"Right." I was surprised at the sudden stab of pain I felt.

"Of course." I stood up, walking back along the path to hide my sudden tears. I hated that just hearing his voice, knowing he was close by, could make me cry. After everything, I hated myself for still caring whether or not his feelings for me had been real.

"Are you okay?" Polly asked, making her way toward me.

I turned to her and nodded, blinking away my tears. "I don't want to leave," I said truthfully.

Polly looked down. "I don't want you to go either."

"I hate running away when there's a chance my siblings are still alive, that they could be saved."

"I understand," Polly nodded. "But you have to trust my father—you have to trust *me*—when we say we will do everything we can to save their lives. But first we have to save yours."

Just then we heard a noise behind us, coming from the woods. We ducked down behind the wall, squeezing each other's hands as we waited, listening as heavy footsteps came closer and then stopped. There was a loud crunching sound, the sound of branches being ripped off.

Slowly I inched upward, peering over the wall. Grazing at the trees by the side of the woods was a tall black-and-white horse.

"Caligula!"

I hurtled over the wall and ran toward her. As I ran my hands through her tangled mane I felt a single tear of joy slide down my cheek. Against all odds she had stayed nearby, as if waiting for me. Tonight I would not leave Balmoral alone. I would take her with me to Wales, and whatever came next.

27

AS POLLY AND I APPROACHED THE CASTLE ON CALIGULA, WE SAW a few hundred men and women standing outside. It was the troops Polly's father had gathered together from the villages. Some held the blacksmith-made weapons Polly had described, while others clutched homemade bows and arrows and swords. They were dressed in their own clothes, a far cry from the uniforms with shining brass buttons worn by the New Guard. My heart sank as I saw how small their ranks were, and I pulled Caligula to a stop. The sky was darkening overhead and the air was damp with oncoming rain. This would be my last hour here.

I thought of the long ride through the night to Wales. The

roadways would be risky: There were bandits and Roamers and, worst of all, Hollister's army. There was no guarantee we would even make it to Wales alive. But at least I had Caligula with me.

Standing on the castle steps, raised above the crowd, stood General Wallace. He had aged rapidly since last year's state dinner at Buckingham Palace. The fall of the government and the death of the king had clearly weighed heavily on him, turning his hair silver-gray and leaving dark shadows under his eyes.

When he saw us coming, the general stepped forward to meet us. "Princess," he said, bowing his head. "I am so sorry."

Clara appeared next to him, and I quickly slid off Caligula to hurry toward her. My heart raced in panic. "Sorry?" I asked, my voice breaking.

Clara pulled me into a hug, her tears falling onto my hair and the back of my shirt. "They've just announced . . . It just came through on the radio . . ." She covered her face and bent over in choking sobs as George hurried to her, still holding a radio with one forlorn-looking, drooping antenna.

"Cornelius Hollister has announced the execution of your brother and sister," he said solemnly. "This Sunday morning."

"I can't believe I lived to see this," the general said quietly to himself. "The end of the house of Windsor." A single tear escaped his eye. Everyone in the army was crying or shouting, waving their arms; everyone except me.

I stood stock-still behind Caligula, who blocked me from the view of the crowd, staring at the radio in cold disbelief. Tears, screams—anything would have been better than standing here frozen, imagining my sister and baby brother with nooses around their necks, their bodies hanging limp against the London skyline while thousands looked on.

Polly wrapped her arms around me, holding me tight. "This is all my fault," she cried. "I told them you were dead. I thought they would leave us alone, but now I've made everything worse. . . ."

"You were only trying to help. You didn't know what would happen." I held Polly's shaking body, trying to comfort her.

I continued to stare at the radio, listening as the broadcaster listed village after town after city after village that Hollister's army had already conquered. Clara and George caught Polly's eye and gestured for her to take me around the side of the castle. Clara held out a small bag of things she had packed for my journey: some warm clothes and a couple sandwiches for me and the general.

"Eliza," George was saying, "we are only doing this for your safety."

I nodded. "It's almost dark," Polly said through her tears.

Clara put her hand on my shoulder. "They'll have food and clothes for you there. Things are better in Wales."

I nodded, biting my lip. I looked up to see the general walking toward me, wearing his army uniform and leading his horse. He carried two guns.

"I'm so sorry," he told me. "I was at all three of your christenings. Your father was a good man, Princess, and it was an honor to serve him." He shook his head slowly, looking up at the darkening sky. "We should get going. We have a long ride ahead of us."

I nodded again. I wanted to say something but my voice had died in my throat.

Polly hugged me so hard I stumbled backward. Clara and George said their good-byes next, but I couldn't look them in the eye. The two people I wanted to say good-bye to the most weren't even there. By the time I reached Wales, they would be dead.

I swung myself up onto Caligula. From her massive height, I could see out over the Resistance troops, who seemed to be disbanding. "What will they do now?" I said to the general.

"Surrender. These people have young children and elderly parents to take care of. They don't want to sacrifice their lives if there is no chance." He looked at me sadly. "I'm so sorry it has come to this, Princess. Even in my wildest nightmares I would have never dreamed I'd live to see the day when England was taken over by a dictator."

I stared out at the disbanding army, the men and women crying, hugging each other good-bye. It was the last hope for England, and now it was over. I was watching the end before it had even truly begun. We were surrendering to Cornelius Hollister's reign of terror.

I held Caligula steady, blinking back tears. I understood their choice. Why should they risk their lives if I wasn't risking mine? As much as they wanted a free England, they wanted to live even more. To spend their lives with the people they loved, their families. That was what I wanted most in the world. Still, there was a voice inside me that screamed, *It isn't over*. Not yet.

I looked down into the general's tired eyes. "With all due respect, General, I cannot follow your orders. I'm not going to Wales. I'm staying, and I will fight, even if that means I'm the only one left."

Polly gasped. A slow line of worry spread across the general's face.

"Eliza, you have to go!" Clara protested. "It's the only way you'll be safe."

"I don't *have* to do anything!" I cried. I thought of Mary standing up to me in the Steel Tower, making the difficult decision when I was unable to. "My sister and brother are imprisoned, which makes me the acting royal. I don't take orders from anyone. Now, you can join me in my fight, or you can surrender to Hollister."

Before anyone could utter another word, I tapped Caligula, cantering in the direction of the soldiers. I threw back my shoulders and looked out over the army, blocking their path as they started to disband. "Please! Wait! I know the risks are great but please, please, don't give up now."

The crowd began to murmur quietly to each other as I approached. The whispers and mutterings crested rapidly.

"It's Eliza Windsor!" one of the women shouted out, pointing from the crowd.

"The princess!"

"She's alive!"

"I am alive," I shouted, "and I won't sit back and watch my beloved country be destroyed. If you're willing to fight, then so am I!"

I locked eyes with several people in the crowd: a mother with a young girl, a father with two boys. "I apologize to all the people of England who were starving in the streets while we had extra food in the palace. We should have invited you in; we should have shared every last morsel." I swallowed, pausing as my eyes scanned the faces in the crowd, still staring up at me. "Please forgive my family. Please forgive me. I never knew what it was like to be hungry, to be homeless, to be alone, but I do now, and I will fight to make sure all of England's citizens never have to go without food or shelter again."

The crowd was silent. My eyes jumped nervously from face to face. Now that I was no longer speaking I could feel the thrum of my heart.

"I am still willing to fight against them," one man shouted, an older farmer. "They burned down my house while my wife was asleep inside—she was killed."

More people joined in with tales of pillage and murder by Hollister's army, until it seemed the whole crowd was shouting.

"If the princess is going to join the troops," the general said, riding over on horseback, "then so am I!"

The army roared in appreciation as they picked up their weapons and held them high.

"Our numbers may be small, our weapons may be old, but we have truth and goodness on our side," I shouted. "The desire to live in a better world. Gather your weapons, those who want to join us, and meet back here at first light. Then we're off to Newcastle!"

28

THE SKY AT DAWN WAS THE COLOR OF ASH. AS WE PREPARED FOR battle the soldiers said farewell to their loved ones. A weeping mother kissed her young daughter good-bye. An elderly father gave his old hunting knife to his teenage son.

I was selfishly glad to see Eoghan, our former stablemaster. His wife had died several years ago, leaving him with two young boys. It pained me to see him leave them in the care of their grandmother while he risked his life in battle, but I was grateful for every familiar face.

A small figure on a russet mare cantered up to me.

"What are you doing here, Polly?"

"I'm coming with you," she said.

"Polly . . ."

"It's my country, too, Eliza. I want to fight." She rode ahead to the frontline troops, where the strongest men were. I couldn't hide my concern. She was so small, a wisp of a girl riding on her fragile mare. I took a deep breath, looking up at the sky. *Please keep her safe*, I prayed. *Please keep them all safe.*

The cool morning air rushed toward us as we rode out into the darkness, headed for the city of Newcastle. The city had the largest number of active, working coal mines in the country, and was located on a strategic river port. Without it, the general explained, it would be much more difficult for Hollister to conquer the north.

We knew that their numbers would be strong, but we had the element of surprise. They could not have foreseen how our army had grown, how many new recruits volunteered at dawn outside the castle gates, eager to join the fight. Still, as I looked back over my shoulder at the troops on horseback, I wished we had more men and women on our side.

Caligula took the lead, the general right behind us. He had mapped out places along the way, villages with inns or wells where we could stop and refuel and let the horses drink. As fair as the weather had been during the day, the night was still cold, the temperature dropping quickly as the sun went down.

I knew we would be outnumbered, but my faith lay in the general's tactics. He was sending partisan troops up ahead to ambush the New Guard's first line of defense, hoping to significantly weaken their forces before the battle at Newcastle.

As we rode out of the tunnel underpass, nearing the town of Baddoch, we saw a band of horsemen in the road. I pulled tightly on Caligula's reins as the army slowed down behind me.

"What's going on?" I asked Eoghan, who had pulled up beside me.

"I don't know, but be prepared to fight." He peered out into the darkness. All that was visible in the road ahead were the yellow flames from the horsemen's lanterns.

"Weapons ready," the general called, and the air filled with the sounds of guns readying for fire, swords being unsheathed, and bows being nocked with arrows. I held my sword steady.

My strength was in riding, but faced with a roadblock of men on horseback, I wasn't sure what tactic to take. Should the troops be charging at them? Or did we take a more peaceful approach?

Eoghan rode slowly on my left, his gun at the ready. "I've got you," he said, turning to me.

"I've got you too," I said, though I was worried.

As we approached the large group on horseback, I mentally prepared myself for the worst. "One first shot, one offensive move, and we charge," the general said in a low voice.

"Stay back," Eoghan said, and I held down Caligula's reins to let Eoghan and the general ride ahead toward the lights.

"Who's there?" the general called out, a hint of worry fraying the edges of his words.

"We came to join the Resistance troops," a figure said. I peered into the darkness and thought I made out a bearded man on a dark horse.

"You're here to join the Resistance?" the general repeated. "Are you armed?"

"We gathered what we could," the man said. "A few of us have guns. Mostly, we have bludgeons welded from metal and some lead pipes."

I rode to the front and took in the group of new recruits. "We are grateful for anything. Please, come join us."

A loud cheer went out from the troops as the new recruits marched forward, swelling our ranks. I pulled Caligula around, looking for Polly. I wanted to see the expression on her face. With the addition of the new volunteers the army had nearly doubled in size.

She was caught in the middle of the swirl of people. Caligula parted them easily, and I pulled her forward with me, reaching over to hug her and feeling once again how small she was. Her ribs protruded through her shirt. I had the awful image of a sevil flying straight through to hit her, and wished I had some kind of armor for her.

George rode up next to her. "Look at all this, Dad," she said, a proud grin on her face. He smiled back weakly, clearly worried about having both Polly and me in combat.

"Quiet, please," the general announced. A hush fell over the troops. "Those of you without weapons or horses," he continued, "can join the partisans, whose job is to distract and divide the enemy however they can. Your weapons will be anything you can come by—ropes, rocks, stolen sevils— but most of all, your brains. We appreciate every last one of you, but it is a dangerous role, and I want you to know the risks before you decide to join us. Unlike Hollister, we don't force anyone into our army."

Another cheer went through the crowd as every last man and woman in the group came to join us.

As we moved south, the same thing happened in every town and village we approached. The old army post of Blackburn yielded a crowd of hundreds, maybe a thousand, all gathered on horseback and armed with guns. In the village of Clavern, most were too young or too old to fight, but they stood by the side of the road, handing us packets of food and canteens of water and cheering us on our way. New recruits gathered in the town centers, at the resting posts at the forks in the road, at crossways and under bridges, in clusters of two or four or twenty. And the numbers began to add up.

On the third morning, the metal arches of the Tyne bridge—a feat of engineering that had survived the Seventeen Days against all odds—were visible in the soft gray light. We had arrived at Newcastle. I looked back over my shoulder at the faces of the men and women, set with determination and united by a single cause, and wondered if we were marching to our deaths.

Once our scouts had surveyed the surrounding landscape and the roads that led into town toward Hollister's army, General Wallace announced that we would split into four groups. We would surround the city on all sides and attack at once, at the sounding of the horn. "Swords out and guns loaded," he said. "Now move quickly—surprise is our greatest advantage!"

Not by accident, Eoghan was in the same group as Polly and me. We descended the hill outside the city quickly, and when we reached the top, Eoghan passed me a pair of binoculars. I could see Hollister's soldiers, mostly still asleep, some beginning to stir the fires and prepare breakfast. They were unarmed, their horses still tethered. Caligula moved uneasily beneath me, and I knew she had sensed that battle was near. "Shhh," I whispered, stroking her neck to calm her down.

And then the horn sounded. It was time to go.

I took a deep breath, loosening the reins and grasping the pommel of my sword tight in my hand. Eoghan nodded and we rushed forward as one. I felt suddenly like I was part of something much bigger than myself, swept along by a fierce tide. I saw shock—and fear—on our enemies' faces as they hurried to find their weapons before our wave of troops crashed over their camp.

A few of them found their rifles and started firing. A bullet cut through the air, missing my head by millimeters and almost clipping my ear. I ducked low, close to Caligula's mane. Her hooves were a blur. As our troops collided with theirs, everything was chaos.

Caligula and I moved like one being. After our long journey to Scotland with me riding bareback, she was so attuned to my small movements and shifts in weight that all I had to do was think something and she seemed to sense it.

She knew when to spin around and when to stay still, leaving me free to focus on the sword in my right hand.

I slashed and parried, always aware of Eoghan on my left and Polly on my right. Eoghan was an incredible shot. He was stealing the weapons of most soldiers he killed, accumulating quite a collection of sevils and pistols.

I looked over toward the tents, where Hollister's army was still in chaos. Most of the warhorses were still tied up—the men must not have had time to saddle them with all their complicated armor and spiked gear. I wanted to release them. It would destroy Hollister's cavalry, and these horses deserved to live like Caligula, free of pain.

Caligula seemed reluctant to move toward them, but she did as I wanted, edging toward the side of the wall where they were lined up. I leaned over and pulled up stake after stake, yanking them out of the earth like tough roots. The horses roared and ran in every direction. One of them, pure white with angry red eyes, turned around to face a soldier carrying a harness toward him and trampled the soldier to death.

Just then one of the soldiers charged toward me, gun in hand. He raised the barrel to aim it directly at my forehead. I grabbed my sword, but I knew I would already be dead by the time I charged him; he was just too close.

Everything happened at once. He fired the gun as Caligula charged forward, rearing up to stab at him with her hooves. She moved faster than I'd ever seen and knocked him backward as the shot rang out somewhere behind my head. He lay in a crumpled heap on the ground, but it looked like he was still breathing. I jumped back on Caligula and spun away, back toward the battle, unable to bring myself to finish him off.

My eyes zeroed in on Polly. She seemed so small and defenseless atop her tall russet mare. Where was Eoghan? I watched her lean over, helping someone who had been knocked to the ground, leaving herself utterly defenseless. I realized it was George. He'd been hurt. I rushed Caligula toward her, sword outstretched.

But another rider was charging toward Polly too. He came up behind Polly, aiming his sevil with perfect precision at the back of her head.

"Polly!" I screamed, but she didn't hear me. I charged forward, swinging at enemies right and left, trying to forge a path through the thick of the battle. All I could think about was getting to Polly.

Just in time, I slid in front of her and blocked the rider's attack. He kept slashing at me, but I parried every hit, fueled by a fierce protectiveness, until one of my blows struck him so hard that he fell backward off his horse.

I looked over at Polly. She was pulling her father up into the saddle, completely oblivious to what had just happened. Even in the midst of everything, I felt a pang of sadness and envy. I wished I could have done the same for my father when he had lain bleeding on the ground.

It was midday when the New Guard retreated, fleeing down the roads toward London. The Resistance forces had suffered some injuries but very few deaths. Exhausted but exhilarated, we set out for London to fight the next battle.

We rode slowly, taking the winding and narrow roads through the woods to avoid the interstate. At each village, groups of people waved at us, cheering us along. Word of our victory had already spread. Everywhere we went, people offered us food, blankets, buckets of horse feed.

We sat on the lawn outside the inn of a small town, surrounded by a buzz of excitement, while the innkeeper passed around cups of water and cold ale. Though I wanted to join in the celebrations, a heaviness anchored me to the ground. I couldn't shake the image of two nooses being placed around the heads of my brother and sister. Today was Wednesday. In a few days' time they would be dead, and Cornelius Hollister would crown himself king.

I felt a tap on my shoulder. A young girl of about five or

six stood in front of me. She was barefoot and wore a dirty white sundress.

"Princess Eliza?" She curtsied, holding up the sides of her dress as she bowed her head. Her blonde hair was so fine the sun shone through it. "This is for you," she said, pulling a small navy blue box from her pocket and holding it out.

I managed a weak smile. "Thank you."

With another curtsy, she walked away, disappearing into the crowd.

I stared down at the small box, curling my fingers around it. My curiosity got the better of me and I opened it. It was a locket, and I gasped as the gold caught the light. It looked identical to the one I had worn for most of my life. My fingers were trembling as I undid the latch, not daring to hope what I would find inside.

A tear pricked my eye and slid down my cheek. I knew this photograph all too well. The long dark hair, the melancholy pale blue eyes. It was my mother.

I looked up after the girl, to ask where she had gotten this, but she was gone. It was impossible—a miracle, really—to think my locket had been traded by the Collectors only to find its way to the Scottish countryside, and back to me. *How?* But as I clasped the locket around my neck, tucking it safely under my shirt, I began to feel the faint stirrings of hope. If my mother's photograph could find its way to me against all odds, then maybe my family could find its way home.

We rode through the day and into the night, joined by more and more volunteers from all over Scotland. Word of the upcoming execution and our recent victory had spread rapidly. By the time we reached the outskirts of London on Friday night, we had gained hundreds, even thousands, of men and women. We had finally formed a real army.

When we rounded a bend in the foothills, I looked back at the line of riders behind me, so long it disappeared in the distance. For the first time I believed we might have a fighting chance.

29

THE NIGHT WAS PITCH BLACK, THE MOON COVERED IN HEAVY clouds that threatened rain. A strong wind blew in from the north, blistering and cold. Far off in the distance over the Northern Hills, streaks of fire lit up the sky, vanishing as they fell. We rode down narrow country lanes through the woods until the general led us to a deserted street of burned and abandoned houses. Loose electrical wires, harmless now, whipped in the gusts of wind. We dismounted, leading our horses through the doorway of what looked like a brick house.

On the entrance wall, a row of coat hooks, each labeled with a child's name, hung over a row of wooden cubbies. I realized we were in an abandoned schoolhouse. The toilets were low and small, the blackboards covered in dust, and rows of small desks and chairs lay broken and toppled. Behind the school was a walled-in garden where the partisan and ground troops had set up sleeping and medical tents for the soldiers.

A white tent stood out among the others, where Clara was tending the wounded. The worst was one man who had been impaled by a sevil. He lay in the tent, gritting his teeth as Clara extracted the bloody rod from his abdomen.

We gathered in the main tent, where mugs of hot water mixed with a few tea leaves were being passed around. General Wallace sat beside the radio. The excitement that had fueled us earlier had turned to exhaustion, and I dreaded what I would hear. A new voice came through the airwaves, a voice I immediately recognized as Cornelius Hollister's.

"Our recent losses at the Battle of Newcastle will not defeat us. The execution of the last remaining Windsors will be held as planned on Sunday morning, followed by my immediate coronation as king of England."

A fearful silence fell over the troops at the words. Even his voice sounded evil; low and menacing.

General Wallace quickly shut off the radio. "Do not let him scare you. We won the Battle of Newcastle and tomorrow we will do the same. We will march into London together and storm the Tower. But for now we must get some rest."

The soldiers retreated to the sleeping area, where they took off their boots and checked their rifles, hiding them beneath their bedding. I lay down beside Polly on a tarp, resting my head on her shoulder. It was a cold night, but the tent stayed warm from the body heat and the fires still burning around camp. Soon the soldiers lay still, breathing heavily in the night.

"You must be so proud of your father," I said to Polly. "He helped start this whole Resistance army."

"I am," she said sleepily. "And I'm proud of you, Eliza. You could be sleeping in a real bed tonight, safe under a real roof. You could have gone to Wales. But you chose to stay and fight."

I stared up at the starless sky, thinking of Mary and Jamie. My greatest fear was that we would arrive too late to save them.

"I wish the British people were more proud of my father," I whispered. I had never spoken these words aloud before and felt an ache in my chest as I said them. "I wish *I* was more proud of my father. His legacy was a shattered country. Even if England survives all this, he will always be remembered as the king who almost lost us everything." I thought of one night last spring, during a meeting of all the heads of government at Buckingham Palace. Mary and I were passing around hors d'oeuvres and glasses of red and white wine—playing hostess. It was our favorite thing to do at the palace parties. An argument erupted between Prime Minister Charles Bellson and my father. The prime minister was trying to warn him of a "mounting problem" while my father sat on the sofa smoking his cigar and sipping vintage wine. "That's preposterous," my father said. "Let's just drop the subject."

The prime minister was trying to convince him to turn over the last of the lands around Balmoral. Father used to call them "Mary's woods." It was said that a supply of oil and cadmium was in the soil, but the woods would be ruined in the digging process. My father stood up, almost teary-eyed. The woods were one of the last properties owned by the royal family and not the state, and letting go of them would be admitting defeat. He was not willing to do that. He turned to the prime minister and said, "Please, you are ruining the party."

Polly squeezed my hand in hers. "He was a good, kind man. He didn't want to start a war. And the Seventeen Days had nothing to do with him. He had no idea what would happen—no one did."

"I know," I said. *Perhaps he was not the best king*, I thought, *but he was a kind man and a good father. It is not just soldiers who are killed in wars*, he used to say, *civilians die, too*. Children, mothers, fathers, grandparents. There is no such thing as a safe war, which was perhaps why he never started one with Cornelius Hollister. "But I wish my family had done more."

"*You* will," Polly murmured. "Mary is going to be a great queen, and you are the best princess this country has ever seen. Now get some sleep. We need to be up in a few hours." She turned on her side, pulling the covers to her chin. Soon I heard the steady sound of her breathing.

I felt exhausted, my body heavy as lead, but when I closed my eyes I found myself unable to sleep. The execution was in a matter of hours. I pulled on the sweater I was using as a pillow and tied my boots, moving carefully so as not to wake Polly. I tiptoed around the other soldiers, stepping over sleeping bodies until I was near the door flap. Every one of them had a beating heart. Every one of them was someone's mother or father, sister or brother, son or daughter. And every one of them was loved deeply, the way I loved Mary and Jamie.

I walked quickly out into the cool night air, taking deep breaths, hoping to walk the worry out of my mind. The battle, the invasion of the Steel Tower, keeping our troops alive, getting Mary and Jamie out. We had won the Battle of Newcastle, but I knew Hollister's real forces were waiting for us in London. I pressed my hands against my face, wishing I could cry. I wanted some kind of relief.

There was a flicker in the dark, the flame of a match moving to light a torch. Eoghan's face appeared out of the darkness. "Are you okay?" he asked, tilting his head at me.

I was glad to see him. "I'm fine," I said, shivering from the cold night air. "I just can't sleep, that's all."

"Here." He placed his coat around my shoulders. "This will keep you warm."

I felt the touch of his hand through the fabric of his coat, warm and reassuring as he sat beside me on the broken stone wall.

"Up worrying?" Eoghan continued. "It happens to me all the time."

I looked over at him. His brown eyes glistened in the dancing light of the torch. "I understand now why my father never wanted to start a war," I said softly. "People are going to be killed tomorrow, people who are loved and respected and *needed*. Because of me."

Eoghan looked away. "When I was young, my mother sent me to Sunday school. They taught us about Heaven and Hell." He pulled his jacket close, his breath visible in the cold night air. "But when my son was born, he was very sick. The doctors told us he wouldn't make it. I held him in my arms, just praying and praying that he would live. For the first week, I hardly let go of him at all. He was so small. I remember thinking, what kind of world is this where you can love someone so much, only to lose them forever? That's when I realized that Heaven doesn't exist in another place, and neither does Hell. It's all here on Earth. We live them both, right here with one another. It's just that sometimes we have to go through Hell to get to Heaven."

His eyes blazed in the firelight. "We are all here because we want to be. Every one of these men and women knows the risks and is willing to die for the cause. For *your* cause. Have faith in our troops, have faith in our country, and most of all, have faith in yourself." He paused. "I know you may not have faith right now. But until you regain yours, trust me when I say *I* know we are doing the right thing."

30

THE GRAY OF THE SKY AND THE GRAY OF THE PAVEMENT BLURRED together in the predawn darkness as we rode silently into London. In the distance, the Steel Tower rose from the city skyline. The general brought us to a halt, straining through binoculars to see what lay ahead on the road to the Tower.

"The roads look clear," he said, but his brow furrowed skeptically. "Hollister's forces seem to be headed south. They're fighting another band of Resistance troops coming in from that way."

I turned to Eoghan and Polly on either side of me. They looked visibly relieved to find out we were not alone. The general had heard on the radio that battles had been fought in the south by other Resistance forces and that Hollister's army had suffered considerable losses. Public opinion seemed to be changing. I felt hopeful, but I knew never to underestimate Cornelius Hollister.

The general gathered the troops, giving final battle instructions. "We will divide into two groups. I'll lead the cavalry to the Tower, the infantry will fight the troops to the south."

I looked behind me at the thousands of troops spreading out like a sea. The Tower was so close. We had come so far.

"I'll stay with you," Eoghan said to me.

"All's clear!" the soldiers on lookout called as they rode toward us.

The general looked back at us. I waited anxiously, trying to read his expression, but he mostly just seemed exhausted. "Charge the Tower!" he finally called.

The brigade of horses made their way across the Thames. The roads were clear, and we rode without opposition toward Tower Bridge. When we arrived at the Tower, we found the drawbridges down. I slowed Caligula. The cavalry were already making their way across, following the general's command to invade the White Tower first. Eoghan disappeared inside, followed by Polly and George, who were among the first to enter.

"Wait!" I called out breathlessly to the troops. The bridge was never left down; something was wrong. "Turn back! Turn back!"

But it was too late. My voice was lost in the sound of horses galloping across the creaking drawbridge. Turning back was no longer an option.

"Caligula, forward." I tapped her with my feet. She sensed my fear of crossing the bridge, but she moved forward, walking gingerly.

Suddenly the bridge began to move beneath our feet. Inside the Tower, alarms echoed, signaling the raising of the bridge. Caligula tried to regain her footing, but the bridge was rising rapidly, and she slipped backward.

I let go of the reins, clasping my arms around her neck instead, trusting her completely. She lowered her forelegs into a crouch and took off, her back legs lurching forward as she jumped across the widening gap. She landed heavily on her front legs and slid down the slope of the other side of the bridge.

We rode through the open gates, past the bell tower, the White Tower, and into the Green Tower, the walled inner garden where throughout history the aristocracy had been executed. I heard a loud clanking sound. Looking behind me, I saw the gates, known as the Traitor Gates, closing shut behind us. We were trapped inside the walls.

I rode up to General Wallace. He was looking frantically back and forth from the Tower to the closed gates. I knew what he was thinking. We needed more troops to win, and to get out alive we'd need an escape route. Without warning, Hollister's men charged from every direction.

I pulled my sword from its sheath as a masked and armored girl on horseback charged at me. She didn't have a sevil, but she raised a long sword, swinging the blade just inches from my neck. Caligula turned and shot past her. There was a violent crack of thunder, and a sudden downpour turned the courtyard into churning mud. The rain fell like a veil, making it difficult to distinguish friends from enemies.

The wounded fell from their horses and ran for cover inside the walls of the Tower. It was a fatal mistake—they would never be able to escape from there. I heard some-one yelling on my right and looked to see the girl in armor charging me again, her blonde hair falling loose under her helmet. *Portia*. I raised my sword above my head, holding it with both hands. Caligula spun around, and as she reared up on her back legs, I stood in the stirrups and brought my sword down hard on Portia's shoulder. The blow barely fazed her; she recovered, raised her sword, and came at me once more.

Polly appeared by my side, knocking into Portia. Her

small brown mare was hardly a match for Portia's warhorse, but she had the element of surprise and threw Portia off balance. Portia's eyes opened in shock as she swerved, falling sideways off her horse.

"Polly!" I cried out. She smiled at me, her whole face lighting up with pleasure. She turned to rejoin the battle just as a dagger flew through the air and sank into her back. Pain and shock blossomed on her face. She reached slowly behind her to feel the dagger with her hand. Her eyelids fluttered closed as she slid to the ground.

I saw the triumphant smile on Portia's face from where she crouched on the muddy ground. I didn't stop to think. There was a loud ringing in my ears, or maybe it was the sound of Caligula's roar as she ploughed forward, charging straight at Portia. I slashed at her with my sword, unsure if I had made contact, my vision red with rage. With a cry of pain, Portia retreated, scrambling backward like a crab. She glared at me when she reached cover.

I didn't have time to pursue her. I jumped off Caligula and ran to Polly's side. She lay in the mud at the edge of the battlefield, her eyes still closed, the color drained from her face and lips. I knelt and lifted her head to my lap. Her skin felt cold and wet from the rain. The dagger had pierced her ribs on the right side. Carefully I withdrew it. Blood seeped out, turning to red water as the rain washed it away.

"Keep breathing," I said, holding her hands in mine. "Keep breathing, Polly, please!"

I yelled for help, screaming into the rain, into the sea of horses and bodies, splattering mud, swords and chains hurtling through the air. But no one came. The rain fell harder now, driving into the ground like bullets. I pulled Polly away from the stampede to a dark corner.

She made a rasping noise as she breathed. I could not let her go. I could not let her die.

"Polly." I tried to warm her hands in mine. "Please, try . . . please try to breathe. I know it's painful. I'm going to get you help." I ran out into the muddy rain-soaked field, searching for one of our soldiers.

"Eliza!" Eoghan raced between me and a soldier wielding a spiked chain. The chain missed me but whipped against Eoghan's back, flinging him forward. He gripped his horse's mane and shot his rifle with the other hand.

"Polly's been badly hurt! We need to get her out of here." Eoghan turned at my words and followed me to the alcove where Polly lay. She was still breathing, but the rasping sound had worsened. I looked out across the battlefield, relieved to see the gates had been broken open.

"Help me lift her onto Caligula," I said.

"I'll take her." Eoghan pulled her onto the front of his saddle and sat behind her. "You follow us."

Across the field, the general was calling to our troops to retreat. Anyone who could escape ran back through the gates. The ground was covered with the bodies of men and women, their uniforms drenched with rain and splattered with mud. It was impossible to tell our troops from the enemy's. Lying mangled and helpless on the ground, we all looked the same.

I hurried after Eoghan toward the gates. Caligula trudged through the mud, her dark mane soaked through. I felt her shiver and knew she was cold and tired, but I pressed my heels into her sides, urging her forward. "Come on, girl," I murmured. Any minute now they would raise the draw-bridge.

Bullets and spears flew past us in the surrounding rain, and I heard the telltale clanking that meant the bridge was being lifted.

"Hurry, Caligula!" I shouted. We were so close, only a few yards away. Caligula tensed to jump, but her left hind leg was moving strangely. I looked back and saw a long gash along her flank. I knew Clara could treat the wound when we got back to camp, so I kept forcing Caligula forward.

But just as she leapt to make the crossing, a rider flew out of the rain toward us, knocking us backward into the Tower.

Caligula let out a roar. I looked to see a spear embedded in her flank.

The rider came toward me. I saw the blond hair, the straight teeth, and raised my sword to swing at him. He blocked my attack, then twisted his wrist, somehow wrenching my sword from my grasp. The next thing I knew I was on the ground, his blade at my throat.

"I want you alive," Cornelius Hollister gasped through gleaming white teeth.

31

"LOCK HER IN THE DUNGEON," HOLLISTER ORDERED HIS MEN. THE guards grabbed me roughly, cuffing my hands behind my back and shackling my feet with chains. They dragged me across the battlefield in the pouring rain. The last thing I saw as they pushed me into the White Tower was Caligula galloping through the closing gates, the spear still protruding from her flank.

The hatchway closed, and the iron grids slammed against the damp stone floor. I was alone in the dungeon, a stone room with a twenty-foot ceiling and no windows.

"She won't be able to get away this time," one of the guards said to another as the sound of their footsteps retreated down the hallway.

I clutched at the bars and shook them in desperation, screaming until my throat was hoarse, but the iron bars were solid, and no one came. Finally, I slid to the damp ground, exhausted. I felt too hollow, too empty to even cry. Mary and Jamie would die soon. The knowledge that I had failed them yet again hit me like a physical blow. All I wanted at this point was to say good-bye.

I curled up on my side, shivering in the cold, and took my locket from around my neck. As I stared at my mother's photograph, I thought about what Eoghan had been trying to tell me about faith. He wanted me to believe in something. *I believe in plenty of things*, I thought with a bitter smile. I believed that I was going to die tomorrow. I believed that Cornelius Hollister was evil. I believed that I would never see my siblings again.

I wasn't sure how much time had passed when I heard the jangling of keys and the pounding of footsteps approaching my cell. I stood up quickly, pressing my face against the bars to peer through the darkness. The small yellow flame of a candle was bobbing down the hallway, growing closer and closer.

"Hello?" I called. "Hello?" I didn't care who it was. I didn't care if they were coming to kill me. I just felt relief knowing that I would see another person before the very end.

The face of a guard appeared in front of the bars, illuminated by the dim light of the candle. He was an older man with gray hair and a leathery face riddled with wrinkles. Without speaking, he unlocked a tiny slot between the grates to pass me a tray of bread and a glass of water.

Then he cleared his throat and, keeping his eyes downcast, read aloud from a piece of paper.

"I come as the official envoy of Cornelius Hollister to inform you that tomorrow morning, you will be executed alongside Mary Windsor and James Windsor. I have come to ask for any last requests." The candle shone on his face.

"Rupert?" I said hesitantly. "Is that you?"

He said nothing, keeping his eyes trained on the paper in his hands. "Rupert," I said again, positive now that it was our butler, a man I had known all my life, "don't you recognize me?"

"I am so sorry," he finally said, raising his eyes to meet mine. "The night they raided the palace they killed my youngest son in front of me. They said if I resisted they would kill my daughter too."

"They killed Spencer?" He was just a child, even younger than Jamie. The two of them had played together in the palace gardens, digging up worms and holding snail races in the shaded grove.

"Your family was so good to me. I wish . . . I wish I could . . ." He shook his head, his voice breaking.

"Rupert, can you bring me to my brother and sister? Please? I just want to say good-bye to them."

Rupert looked at me through the bars. The candlelight flickered against the gray stone walls. He shook his head and started to turn away.

"I'm sorry," I said softly. I stared at his back. "I'm sorry that helping my family has cost you yours."

He paused, and then he turned around. "I can try, Princess," he said finally. "I can't promise anything, but there are others like me, who remain loyal to the king, and to the free government."

"Please, yes, please try," I begged, my voice breaking. "Thank you, Rupert."

He unlocked the door and led me through the damp, mazelike tunnel that led to the White Tower, through the Cradle Tower, and finally into the Steel Tower, where three armed wardens watched the entranceway. They looked at me in surprise.

"Sirs," Rupert said, as we approached the men, "I must speak with you for a moment." The two younger guards looked to the older warden, who seemed to be in charge. He nodded, and Rupert leaned in to murmur something in his ear. He nodded again, slowly. I thought I saw pity in his eyes. "Eliza Windsor will come with me." His voice was shaky with age, and kind.

The other two backed away as the guard led me up the staircase to the top of the tower. I thought of the last time I had been up these stairs, when I sneaked up here after the girl with Mary's teacup. I was full of hope, so very certain that I would rescue Mary and Jamie and that we would all be free. How foolish I had been to think a girl like me could outwit a sadistic dictator and his army of thousands.

Our footsteps echoed on the metal stairway as we made our way up and up and upward still. All the other cells that we passed, cells that had been full to bursting, were empty now. Cornelius Hollister had already executed the other prisoners. He was saving us for last. Grimly, I imagined how he would kill Jamie first, then me, then as his grand finale, he would kill Mary, England's true queen.

Then he would climb Tower Green and place the royal crown upon his head, the crown that I had helped steal. Wearing my family's crown, he would raise his arms, proclaiming himself king of England, while our royal blood dripped down the scaffold onto Tower Green.

32

THE GUARD'S CANDLE HAD BURNED DOWN ALMOST TO THE WICK BY
the time we finally reached Mary and Jamie's cell. They sat
huddled together at the small table, a plate of food in front of
them, but they were not eating. In an act of ironic generosity,
the plate was filled with luxuries: cheese and fruit and soft
bread. This was their last meal.

I paused for a moment at the top of the stairs, watching
them in disbelief. Maybe it was a trick of the light, but Jamie
looked . . . healthy. His cheeks, which just a few weeks ago
had been sunken and hollow, now appeared round and full.
His hair had grown thick and shining. He sat up straight at
the table, talking animatedly with Mary.

"Remember when Dad took us fishing to try to catch dinner and all we caught were minnows?" Jamie laughed.

Mary looked up, her eyes glistening. She looked better, too, like she had been sleeping. "And what about the time when you wanted the toy car for Christmas, and Eliza and I wrapped it in about twenty boxes so you kept unwrapping one after another?"

"That car is still on the shelf in my room. . . ." Jamie's voice trailed off. "What do you think happened to our house? Do you think the whole palace burned?"

"Good memories, good memories only," Mary said, like a teacher to a student, squeezing his hand.

I couldn't help but smile. Even on the last night of our lives, Mary was still the protective, bossy, loving older sister, always determined to make good from the bad. This was why she would have been a great queen. In her reign she would have found a way to restore the crops, to rebuild the cities— to fix what was broken.

When I turned to the guard, I could see him wiping away a tear. He unlocked the cell to let me in.

Mary and Jamie looked up, their eyes wide with surprise. "Eliza?"

"I'll let you have some time to yourselves. God bless you

all." The guard looked like he might say something else. He hesitated, as though considering whether to leave the lock open, giving us a chance to escape. But then he turned the key with a sigh, and the bolt slid into place.

Mary stared at me, stunned. "We thought you were dead."

Jamie ran into my arms, knocking me backward so that we fell together in a heap on the floor. Mary came over and hugged us both.

"Mary, Jamie." My eyes moved back and forth between them. "What happened?" I reached out to touch Jamie's face, his hair, in wonder. His skin felt warm, not cold and clammy as it usually did. "You look so healthy!"

Mary and Jamie shared a silent look. "What?" I asked. "What is it?"

Mary put her fingers over her lips, indicating that I should be quiet. She went to the door of the cell and peered out through the bars. The guard wasn't far off, but his back was to us.

"We promised we would never tell."

"He said he would be killed if anyone found out," Jamie said.

"Who would be killed?"

Jamie went over to the thin mattress on the floor and

pulled back the piece of muslin he had been given for a blanket. He put his hand beneath it and pulled out an amber-colored glass vial, full of small white pills.

He pressed the vial into my hand. "It's an antidote for dark-star poisoning."

Dark star. It was what poisoned my mother when she was pregnant with Jamie. I stared at the bottle in disbelief. All these years there had been a remedy and we hadn't known. On the label in tiny pinpoint letters was written C. H. LABORATORIES. Of course Cornelius Hollister, the man who invented dark star, had also invented a cure for it.

"Who gave this to you?" I asked.

"One of the soldiers."

"Which one?"

"He never told us his name," Mary said. "He wasn't one of the regular soldiers. He came just once, to give us the medicine."

"Do you remember what he looked like?"

"It was too dark to see. He left it in the night while we were sleeping. I just heard something drop through the door slot."

I stared at the bottle. "Why would he have given you the cure when he knew we were going to die anyway?" I said aloud, then immediately regretted it.

"Eliza!" Mary said in a harsh whisper. Her eyes went to Jamie, healthy at last, but unable to live to enjoy it.

"Well, it's true," I said helplessly, pressing my face into my hands. For the first time in his life, Jamie was healthy. We were all three together. And in the morning we would all die together.

"I'm sorry," I stammered. "It just seems so unfair. So cruel." I stopped myself from saying anything else.

Mary bit her top lip, a habit of hers when she was nervous or trying to make a decision. "Eliza, what happened? We overheard one of the soldiers say that you escaped the Tower, and then they said you were dead."

I sat between them on the bed, all of us holding hands. They listened intently as I told them of diving off the top of the Tower—Mary cried out at that—of riding north on Caligula, of raising the Resistance army and marching back to London. Finally I told them about our failed attack on the Tower that morning.

"The last thing I saw was Caligula escaping just as the gates shut. I hope Polly makes it," I said, squeezing Mary's hand.

The candle flame sputtered out and the cell went dark. From far away came the echoing sounds of footsteps patrolling the Tower. Jamie laid his head on my shoulder and I closed my eyes, breathing in the scent of his hair. I felt my lip quiver, my eyes blur with tears, but I forced myself to think of happy things.

"Do you think there really is a Heaven?" Jamie asked, his small voice floating up into the darkness.

I lay still, afraid to answer, because I wasn't sure.

"Yes, Jamie," Mary said. "And tomorrow we'll see Mum and Dad."

"And Bella," I added. "She'll bark the second she sees you."

Jamie giggled. To laugh at our own death seemed strange, but it was all we could do. I turned over on my side. Jamie's hand lay across my back, and I felt the steady rise and fall of his chest. I looked over to see if Mary was asleep. Her eyes were closed, her mouth slightly open as she breathed softly. Even in sleep she had a composed, dignified look on her face.

I leaned forward, kissing Mary on the forehead, then Jamie. Now I was finally free to cry. I hid my face in the blanket to muffle my sobs.

We used to say our prayers every night when we were younger, and now I heard myself saying them once more. "God bless the people I will leave behind: Polly, George, Clara . . ." As I spoke, I thought of all the dead bodies piled in the courtyard. "Please, God, let Eoghan see his sons again.

274

Let Polly live. Let her mother and father find safety. Please watch over the general, and all the soldiers. And dear God, keep us together in Heaven with our mother and father. And thank you for the life I have had. Amen."

33

THEY BLINDFOLDED US AT DAWN. I NEVER SAW THE FACES OF THE soldiers who came to take us; I only heard their voices. They were not mean or rough, just efficient as they prepared us for our death.

One of the men, with a low voice and hands that smelled of cigarette smoke, told us to stand with our hands behind our backs. When he tied my wrists together his skin felt like sandpaper.

There was the rattle of keys, the cell door opening. "Mary, Elizabeth, James," the man said, lining us up in birth order. They marched us through the hallway and down the spiral staircase. The guard gripped my wrist so tightly I began to lose feeling in my fingers.

"Careful, Jamie," I whispered. I was about to remind him to hold the banister when I remembered his hands were tied.

Unable to see, I took small steps. I had a vivid memory of a time when Bella, still a puppy, had chased a stick onto a frozen pond. I tiptoed out onto the ice to get her. The way I was walking now, as though I was afraid the floor would break beneath me, reminded me of how I'd stepped across the frozen ice.

I heard Mary ahead of me. Even now, she moved with a queen's elegant, even footsteps. Of all of us, she'd had the clearest vision of her future and the life she was now being forced to give up. I thought of how often she used to say, "When I'm married," or "When I'm queen," or "When I have children . . ." She used to keep a list of her favorite names, one for boys and another for girls. Today, she would not scream or break her composure. She would stay strong. Dying with grace wasn't exactly something we had been taught in our royal etiquette lessons, but Mary had lived like a queen for eighteen years, and I was certain she would die like one.

I wondered what they would say about us someday when children reached our chapter in their history textbooks. Were we really the last of the true British monarchy?

At the bottom of the staircase the air smelled like stone

and cold rain. The doors opened and I felt the cool relief of fresh air on my face. I felt a drop of rain on my cheek, then another drop on my forehead.

My stomach clenched in sudden fear. This was the last time I would be able to take in the smells and sensations of early morning or feel the rain on my face. After everything that had happened, everything I had suffered and fought for, I couldn't believe it had come down to this final, sightless walk. What had been the purpose of my too-short life? I had been a daughter, a sister, a friend. Was that enough? My mother always said the most important thing in life was to love and be loved. I had done both.

"Come along." I felt the guard nudge me forward.

"Wait." I steadied myself enough to slip my feet out of my shoes, stepping onto the dewy grass, which felt soft and prickly at the same time. I needed to feel the grass beneath my feet one last time.

"I want to run," Jamie said, his voice rising hopefully. "Please."

"No running," the guard responded sternly.

"Please let him," Mary pleaded. "He's been ill his whole life, until now."

I heard the second guard shuffle his feet and whisper something to the first. I wished I could see their faces. "All right," the first guard reluctantly agreed. "Three minutes. We'll take off your blindfold so you don't trip," he added gruffly.

I couldn't see Jamie, but I heard the patter of his feet, the joy in his voice as he cried out in happiness. Moved, the soldiers let him play for much longer than three minutes. And for once in his life, Jamie got to run outside like a normal boy, as the rain fell harder and the Tower chimed the hour of our execution.

"Remove their blindfolds." I immediately recognized the voice of Cornelius Hollister.

As my blindfold was pulled off I looked around at Tower Green, full to bursting with Hollister's army. I saw some familiar faces: Portia and Tub, dressed up for the occasion. Sergeant Fax, his chest swelling with greedy satisfaction. And standing in uniform among the front line of the soldiers, Wesley. I let my eyes rest on him. I was sure he would turn away in shame, but he met my gaze without blinking. I thought of the careful way he helped treat my wounds in the cottage, the feel of his arms around me. And in that moment I knew that our time together had been true. I did not regret it. He was born into his family just as I had been born into mine, and in the end, he deserved my forgiveness.

Guards led us to our places on the gallows. Three thick nooses hung before us, swaying lightly in the breeze. A man wearing a mask and cape stood on the side of the scaffold, next to a lever. The wooden floor beneath my feet felt hollow. I looked down to see that it was a trapdoor. A horse and old wooden cart were tethered to the scaffold. In a few minutes it would carry our lifeless bodies to the graveyard.

Hollister turned to the crowd, raising his hands for silence as he listed the accusations against us. Apparently we had been guilty of treason, the destruction of liberty . . . As he addressed his army, I tuned out his words and studied him more closely. He was dressed up in a dark commander's uniform, adorned with medals he had awarded himself. He smiled that white, pointed smile that hadn't changed since the day he delivered the deadly fruit to my mother. His face had grown older, deepened with lines, and his hair had grayed slightly at the temple, but his smile was the same, and his blue eyes blazed in satisfaction.

"Bow your heads and say your final prayers," he ordered. As much as I wanted to whisper good-bye, I didn't think I could bear to look at my brother and sister right now. I kept my eyes studiously forward, ignoring the jeering crowds.

A flock of ravens circled the gallows. There was a legend that if the ravens left the Tower, the crown would fall and

Britain with it. But they were not flying away: They circled the crowds, perching on the rooftops and railings like spectators with the best views.

As the executioner looped the nooses over our necks, Mary refused to bow her head or pray. She stared ahead, her chin level, her eyes steady. Not a single tear fell from her eyes. From far away she must have looked strong, but I could feel her trembling beside me.

Jamie bowed his head. "Mummy, Daddy, I can't wait to see you in Heaven. In Heaven where we'll be happy and safe and healthy . . ." Tears rolled down his cheeks, mixing with the rain falling all around us.

The executioner placed his black-gloved hand on the lever. The ropes tightened, pulling up on our necks. I rose onto my tiptoes, hoping it would ease the sudden fiery pain that shot along my nerve endings. Any second now, the trapdoor would open and everything would go dark.

I saw a flash of red, and I thought I was already dying. But my feet were still on the trapdoor. I heard a man roar out in agony and opened my eyes. The executioner lay facedown in the mud, a dozen arrows protruding from his back as though he were a human pincushion.

And then Wesley was on the scaffold, lifting me to loosen the rope as he pulled the noose away from my neck.

I stumbled forward, my vision dancing with black spots. He started to untie my wrists but I shoved him away, nodding mutely at Mary and Jamie. He needed to save them first.

At that exact moment Hollister grabbed the lever, holding my siblings' fate in his hands once more.

34

WESLEY DOVE FOR THE LEVER. I HESITATED BETWEEN MARY AND
Jamie, uncertain which way to go first. My hesitation lasted
less than a second, but it felt like an eternity. Jamie looked
at me, his eyes wide with terror, when Mary snapped to
attention.

"Save Jamie!" she cried, breaking my trance. I ran to my
brother, lifting him in my arms to loosen the noose around
his neck. My fingers fumbled, trembling, as I struggled to pull
the rope through the knot. I wished for a blade so I could just
cut through it. I glanced down to where Hollister and Wesley
were fighting for control of the lever. Wesley strained against
his father, using all his strength to keep it from being lowered.

I freed the noose from Jamie's neck, then hurried over to Mary. The lever went slightly up and down, and the noose pulled on Mary's neck. Her face turned a deep red as she gasped for breath. I tried to run to her side, but someone held me back, knocking me to the ground and pressing his boot down on my stomach. It was Sergeant Fax, his lips turned down in an angry scowl.

"Kill her!" Hollister shouted at Fax, gasping for breath as he continued to fight Wesley.

"Gladly." Fax grinned, reaching for his sevil. I tried to scramble away, but his boot was pushing me down with all of his body weight and I couldn't escape. Just as he raised the sevil, a raven swooped down, fluttering in his face. "What the—" He stumbled backward, off the side of the platform, pulling me with him.

I rolled away as we fell and heard the army erupt into a sudden roar. I sat up and looked around me.

The Resistance forces had arrived.

General Wallace had crashed through the front gates and was marching the cavalry into Tower Green while the foot soldiers scaled the outer wall using ropes and picks.

I turned to climb the stairs to the gallows, struggling to see in the now-pouring rain, but Fax was close behind me. Wesley and Hollister were still fighting on the other side of the platform. The executioner's body had been shoved to the side. I raced over, searching the dead man for a sevil. All I found was a short knife. It would have to do.

I spun around just in time to block Fax's wild, swinging attack. I risked a glance up at Mary. An arrow protruded from her side, blood spilling out to darken her red dress. Jamie struggled to help her, but he could not lift her limp body enough to release the noose. *She's dead*, I thought. *Mary's dead.*

I kept fighting with Fax, my muscles straining to hold the knife against the much stronger sevil. Out of the corner of my eye, I saw a dark-haired soldier on horseback break away from the Resistance forces to charge across Tower Green. As he rode closer I realized it was Eoghan. He leapt from his horse onto the scaffold and severed the rope in a single stroke. At that moment, I gathered all my strength to shove Fax backward and turned to race up the stairs to the platform.

Mary lay crumpled on the ground. She was so still, her face white as a sheet. Jamie sat beside me and took Mary's cold hand in his.

"Is she breathing?" I cried.

Eoghan gathered her in his arms. He felt her throat with his fingers, checking for a pulse. The rain fell heavily around us, beating down like a shower of bullets. There was blood coming from Mary's side where the arrow still stuck out at a strange angle. I could see now that she was breathing, but shallowly.

Eoghan carefully pulled out the arrow, then tore a strip of cloth from his shirt and held it tightly to her wound. I looked at the cloth helplessly; it was already stained pink with blood.

"I'll take her to Clara." Eoghan swung back onto his horse, then reached out to take her in his arms. Her head snapped back, then down again on her chest, like a ragdoll's. Eoghan wrapped his arm tight around her chest as he took the reins in his other hand, charging across the rain-drenched battlefield to the gates.

Jamie and I ran down the scaffold and hid beneath the cart that should have already been wheeled away with our dead bodies. All I had was the knife, and while I trusted myself with it, I wasn't ready to risk Jamie's life. It would be safer to hide.

The ground had turned to mud and the drumming of the rain washed out the sounds of the battle. As Hollister's army fought the Resistance in the Tower Green, Wesley fought his father on the scaffold.

"You know the penalty for treason," Hollister snarled, pointing his sword at his son's throat.

"I'm no traitor," Wesley spat back. "It's you who has

betrayed England. You're a murderer, and now the people aren't afraid of you anymore. You can kill me, but it's too late. The people will keep fighting and will eventually defeat you."

"That's the guard who gave me the antidote," Jamie whispered, pointing to Wesley. "I remember his voice."

Hollister's hand shook with rage as he swung his sword in full force at his son. Wesley stepped back, blocking the stroke with his sevil. His father lunged forward again, slashing Wesley's hand. His sevil tumbled to the ground.

I squeezed Jamie's hand, but he pulled away, running from our hiding place out in front of the scaffold.

"Jamie, no!" I screamed, but he had already darted out to where Wesley's sevil had fallen in the mud. He picked it up and ran around to the other side of the platform. I sprinted after him.

"I never thought I would have to kill my own son," Hollister said, but he didn't sound sad.

At that exact moment, Jamie sneaked up behind Hollister and tossed Wesley his sevil. In a single fluid motion, Wesley caught the blade, whipping it through the air to knock Hollister's sword from his hands. Suddenly the sevil was pressed against Hollister's throat, pinning him to the scaffold wall.

"Go ahead," growled Hollister. "Or do you not even have the courage to finish what you started?"

Wesley stepped back but kept the sevil trained on Hollister's throat. "This is Eliza's choice," he said, surprisingly calm. "She is the one who deserves to avenge her parents' deaths."

I swallowed my fears, picking up the sword from the ground and attempting to steady my trembling hands. I pushed the tip of the sword, Hollister's own sword, toward his heart. I had fantasized about revenge for so long, the anger boiling in me so intensely I thought I would burst with it. But now that the moment was finally here, I felt strangely cheated. Killing him would not bring my parents back. Enough people had died in this war.

I lowered the sword.

"Tie him up," I commanded, and four of the general's soldiers appeared to cuff his hands and feet. I never took my eyes from Hollister's. "You can spend the rest of your life at the top of the Tower, thinking about the people you have killed."

The general led Hollister away, toward the Steel Tower, just as the last of Hollister's army escaped through the gate. I glimpsed Portia slipping away, her hair billowing behind her, followed by a bloodied Sergeant Fax.

The rain continued to fall on the deserted Tower Green. Two nooses hung from the gallows, swaying back and forth in the wind. I watched as the ravens settled in the rooftop gables, snug in their nests of twigs and straw. I couldn't believe it. It was over. After all those months, all the blood and death and heartache, it was over.

Wesley took my hands in his.

"I'm so sorry," he began slowly. "When I woke up that morning and you were missing, I knew exactly where you'd gone. I went back to camp for a horse, and Portia followed me. I think she suspected what was going on." He paused, looking down sadly. "And then I saw you on the roof . . . I never meant for that to happen."

"I know." I shivered, whether from cold or relief or something else entirely, I wasn't sure. "I know that now."

Wesley wrapped his arms around me, and when I didn't pull back, he tentatively leaned in to touch his lips to mine. I felt something flickering, a curl of fire inside me, keeping me warm in the ice-cold downpour.

There was a tug on my sleeve. A soaked Jamie stood shyly beside us.

"Eliza, can we get out of the rain?" he asked, shielding his eyes from the drops.

Wesley dropped his hands to my waist as I reached for

Jamie, hugging him close. I looked up at the sky, the rain falling in my eyes. "Thank you," I whispered to whoever was listening.

We were alive.

Epilogue

IT WAS A PERFECT SUMMER DAY. WISPS OF CLOUD CROSSED THE pale blue sky, while a slight breeze blew through the grasses in the warm sunlight. An outdoor festival was being held in the village square to celebrate Mary's coronation and to thank the townspeople of Balmoral for their support.

There was a maypole for the children, along with an apple dunk and a juggling clown, and Scottish bagpipers and fiddlers and dancing. Horses and donkeys, their manes brushed and braided with gold ribbons, stood in a ring for the village children to ride. I smiled at the sight of Caligula, a full head taller than the other horses, carrying three children on her back and tolerating several others as they combed her tail. The church had been repainted since Hollister's army had tried to burn it down, and it gleamed white in the sun.

Tents had been set up in the square in case of rain, but there was no chance of that today. Rows of long tables spilled over, piled high with homemade pies and scones, fresh-baked breads and cheeses, cold cider and even some long-forgotten delicacies. People had traveled for miles for this celebration.

In her first act as queen, Mary had donated the royal lands to the British farmers. All over England, fresh crops had been planted to feed the nation. The masses were no longer starving. Most important, Cornelius Hollister was securely locked away in the Steel Tower, his army disbanded.

Mary greeted her people with open arms. The arrow wound still caused her pain, and though she tried to hide it, I sometimes saw her wince before catching herself and covering it with a gracious smile. Eoghan was constantly at her side, dark-haired and tall in his navy summer suit. His two young sons played at the maypole while he and Mary looked on.

After Hollister's arrest, Wesley and I had traveled back to the cottage where Nora and Rita lived. We found them tired and thin, skeletons of their former selves, living off weeds and the remains of the canned goods they had stored away. We brought them to Balmoral and set them up in the small gardener's cottage, a new house free of the nightmarish memories of that night. But I never told them I had been there.

I stood in a patch of sunlight on the lawn watching Wesley and Jamie play soccer, Jamie finally learning the tricks of the game he had never been able to play. My eyesight blurred with tears as he laughed and ran, kicking the ball with abandon. Why was it that the happy things now brought tears to my eyes? But I did not want to cry today. I stood up, heading over to the food-laden tables.

Polly, Clara, and George were gathered around General Wallace, who was recounting stories of the war planes he had flown many, many years ago. Clara sat drinking a glass of lemonade, wearing a new dress she had sewn. I recognized the fabric, the small purple flowers against the pale blue background. It had once been a curtain in Polly's bedroom.

Polly walked over to me. She had put her hair up on either side with combs and wore a white-and-yellow sundress that had once belonged to Mary.

"You look pretty," I said.

"So do you."

My hair had grown to just below my ears, and even the scar on my cheek was fading.

"Did you see that chocolate cake over there? I'm dying for a piece."

I grabbed her hand. "Let's get some." We walked over, staring in awe at the round, three-layer cake. I couldn't remember the last time I had eaten chocolate. It was such a rarity.

As we cut a slice to share, I noticed a young boy carrying a blue-and-white bowl of strawberries. He looked about five or six years old and was dressed in a pair of overalls.

"Just look at those strawberries!" Polly cried, her mouth full of cake. "Wherever did you find them?" She stared down into the bowl as though looking at a beautiful work of art.

The bright red color of the berries and their gorgeous, waxy sheen was utterly mouthwatering—but there was also something strange about them. I picked one up, then another, then a third. Each berry was exactly the same, as though they had been cast from a mold.

Polly held a strawberry to her lips, opening her mouth to bite it.

"Polly, wait! No!" I screamed, knocking it forcefully out of her hands. A tinge of pink stained her lips.

"What?" she cried out, frightened by the panic she saw in my eyes.

I quickly snatched up a napkin and wiped the juice from

her lips like a mother would to a child. Taking my thumb and forefinger, I broke open the berry. The inside was full of tiny metal stars. I dropped the berry to the ground, turning to run after the boy. I stepped outside onto the crowded green, looking for the blue of his overalls, the white-blond hair, but I didn't see him in the mass of people dancing and drinking and playing music. The sunlight hit my face and I shielded my eyes, but I already knew that I would find no sign of him.

The boy was gone.

Acknowledgments

I FEEL VERY GRATEFUL TO HAVE BEEN GIVEN THE OPPORTUNITY to write this book. The first person I'd like to thank in this process is Dan Ehrenhaft, for his continued encouragement and for bringing me to Alloy.

I am forever thankful to Josh Bank, Sara Shandler, and Joelle Hobeika for trusting me to fulfill their vision of *The Last Princess*.

I could not have been luckier than to be paired with Joelle Hobeika for this book. This was a true collaboration between editor and writer. Joelle is the kind of hands-on old-fashioned editor people say no longer exist. Her edits beautifully sculpted this book. Her encouragements pushed the story further and her critiques were always exactly right.

And I could not have asked for a better editor than Cindy Eagan at Little, Brown. Cindy's vision and foresight transformed the world of the story and the arc of the plot. I am so happy that we will all be working together again.

A huge thanks to Katie McGee at Alloy for her help, especially recapturing the lost details.

Thanks to my agent, Kim Witherspoon, and Inkwell Management.

Steve Stone, for the beautiful cover art.

Lauren Singer, for her intelligent comments and pre-edit edits on early drafts of the manuscript.

Anna VanLenten, for her continued friendship and encouragement.

To Simon Sher at Northampton Martial Arts, for instructing me on sword fighting strategies and fighting techniques.

To Anabel Mehran, for friendship and the photograph.

Lots of love to Sam, Rowan, and Tess, for understanding the days spent at the library.

My family: my grandmother, Polly Smith; my mother, Sophy Craze; my brother, Jett Craze; my father, Edward Craze; and my wonderful stepmother, Victoria Craze. Thank you to Carol and Allen Shiff. To Fred, Sally, Peter, Christina, and Alexandra Brumbaugh, for their enthusiasm.

To Isabella Rose Lederman and Chianna Li Cohen, my neighbors, for reading early drafts and encouragement.

Where stories bloom.

poppy

Visit us online at
www.pickapoppy.com